Remarks from the Judges

"Judging the prize felt a little like getting back to my roots. It brought me back to that organic and creative place, of being exploratory and experimental. It was shocking to me not just how well written these stories were, but how powerfully the writers' essential selves were coming through. It's almost unbelievable that these are debut stories, because it wasn't easy for me back when I was learning to do this."
—NANA KWAME ADJEI-BRENYAH,
2021 judge and author of *Friday Black*

"One of the things I'm always looking for in literature is a compassionate imagination that portrays a worldview. All these stories were vast in what they were able to imagine and make believe on the page. I am so proud of these stories and so excited to see this book on a shelf."
—KALI FAJARDO-ANSTINE,
2021 judge and author of *Sabrina & Corina*

"I loved the individual stories, and the collection as a whole is even more amazing. The book is a showcase of the many things a short story can do and be: each one drops you into a world that runs by its own rules. You can end up taking a cab ride with strangers or visiting a cemetery with family or having an experience you can't quite assimilate. Drawing on a range of forms and diversity of voices, these stories are vivid and emotionally complex—a celebration of the short story as a form."
—BETH PIATOTE, 2021 judge and
author of *The Beadworkers*

"The short fiction I love best knows how to declare with beauty, 'I prefer not to.' It takes the page as a space to refuse what tends to be, unzipping barriers. This collection gathers stories from voices throwing rice at the moment the essential and the original meet."

—TRACY O'NEILL, 2020 judge and
author of *Quotients* and *The Hopeful*

"I love the stories we picked for this collection. I love their passion, invention, and wildness. I love that these are the artists' first published stories. Your first published story never quite gives up its place in the mind. It was the first one *chosen*—hooray! And yet there is always the nagging doubt ('Is it actually good?') and here we are, celebrating, saying, 'Yes, yes, it is good, so *so* good!'"

—DEB OLIN UNFERTH, 2020 judge and
author of *Barn 8* and *Wait Till You See Me Dance*

"The stories and writers here represent a wide range of voices at the levels of ethnicity, gender, and style. Many carry a very quiet confidence that is refreshing in our harried world, and I feel certain that we will see these authors' names in print again soon."

—NAFISSA THOMPSON-SPIRES, 2020 judge and
author of *Heads of the Colored People*

"I was really inspired by what I saw here—not just the beautiful weirdness of the writers and their work, but the fact that the stories were published. It made me feel so hopeful."

—CARMEN MARIA MACHADO, 2019 judge and
author of *Her Body and Other Parties*

"I was so blown away by the pieces we chose for this collection—there was a wonderful array of different styles and approaches in the submissions we received, but each of the stories we ended up choosing had something startlingly alive and bracingly imaginative within it. You can tell that these are writers working with total dedication to gift these fictive worlds to their readers, to make these surprising, vivid scenarios real. I am so wildly enthusiastic about what these writers are going to do next—and in reading this anthology, you get to say you've followed their entire career, from the very first short story on! You can't beat that."

—ALEXANDRA KLEEMAN, 2018 judge and author of
Intimations and *You Too Can Have a Body Like Mine*

"When I sit down with a short story, I'm hoping to be surprised, or unnerved, or waylaid. I want to feel that something is at stake: in the language and structure, in the emotional lives of the characters, in the consequences of their actions. The best stories are almost otherworldly in their dimensions, as if I have opened a small suitcase left on my front door, only to find three geese, a small child, a jewel thief, and her mother emerging. The stories here delighted and surprised and moved me—I'm so very, very glad that I got to read them and that now you do too."

—KELLY LINK, 2017 judge, 2018 MacArthur Fellow,
and author of *Get in Trouble*

"There were very well written stories that didn't end up on the final list, edged out by the magnitude of feeling and creativity contained in the final twelve. I was particularly struck by the authors' ability to hit it out of the park, first time up. When I read I'm always (like it or not) guessing what's going to happen at the end of the line, the scene, on the plot level. The stories we chose were those that forced me, a relentless overthinker, to stop thinking.

"Amy Hempel's first short story was 'In the Cemetery Where Al Jolson Is Buried.' That story is great, and contains many of the elements she's famous for, but it is not like most of her stories. It's way longer, for one, and more traditional. As if she was only able to peel her inhibitions as she wrote more and more. I'm excited for these authors to participate in that same kind of peeling that helps voice grow more substantial, and I hope this honor gives them the confidence to get weirder and weirder, stronger and stronger."

—MARIE-HELENE BERTINO, 2017 judge and
author of *Parakeet* and *2 A.M. at The Cat's Pajamas*

"A lot of people talk about how so many short stories are becoming too workshopped, too MFA, too a certain kind of story. And I can say, after reading all the entries here, they are wrong. There are so many stories being told that are extraordinary and unexpected. I fretted over picking only twelve. But the stories that won were all stories that astounded us all."

—NINA McCONIGLEY, 2017 judge and
author of *Cowboys and East Indians*

Praise for PEN America
Best Debut Short Stories 2020

"While serving as a fresh, delightful collection of short fiction that looks to our literary future with promise, *Best Debut Short Stories* serves as a timely exploration of an array of themes that speak to our current reality." —CADE JOHNSON, *ZYZZYVA*

"Another slate of outstanding stories from emerging writers of short fiction . . . An anthology full of promise." —*Kirkus Reviews*

Praise for PEN America Best Debut Short Stories 2019

"These stories all share a sense of necessity and urgency . . . What consistently runs through all 12 entries in *PEN America Best Debut Short Stories 2019* is the promise of clear new voices, powerful testimonies, and unique perspectives to assure us that even in our current dark times there will always be the short narrative to take us back into the light." —CHRISTOPHER JOHN STEPHENS, *PopMatters*

"Prominent issues of social justice and cultural strife are woven thematically throughout 12 stories. Stories of prison reform, the immigrant experience, and the aftermath of sexual assault make the book a vivid time capsule that will guide readers back into the ethos of 2019 for generations to come . . . Each story displays a mastery of the form, sure to inspire readers to seek out further writing from these adept authors and publications." —*Booklist*

Praise for PEN America Best Debut Short Stories 2018

"The PEN America contest for outstanding debut fiction returns with a second annual anthology of remarkable prose. This year's submissions were judged by an all-star trio of fiction writers: Jodi Angel, Lesley Nneka Arimah, and Alexandra Kleeman. Once again, the gathered contest winners are uniquely gifted writers whose stories represent literature's bright tomorrow. The pieces showcase a wide breadth of human experiences, representing numerous racial, ethnic, and cultural identities . . . Sharp, engrossing, and sure to leave readers excited about the future of the craft."   —*Booklist*

"These dozen stories tend to the dark side, with rare moments of humor in a moody fictive landscape; they're thus just right for their time . . . A pleasure for fans of short fiction and a promise of good things to come from this year's roster of prizewinners."

—*Kirkus Reviews*

Praise for PEN America Best Debut Short Stories 2017

"Urgent fiction, from breakout talents."   —*Booklist*

"A welcome addition to the run of established short story annuals, promising good work to come."   —*Kirkus Reviews*

"A great overview of some of the year's most interesting fiction."
—*Vol. 1 Brooklyn*

BEST DEBUT SHORT STORIES 2021

Catapult   New York

Edited by Yuka Igarashi and Sarah Lyn Rogers

Best Debut Short Stories 2021

The PEN America Dau Prize

Judges

Nana Kwame Adjei-Brenyah

Kali Fajardo-Anstine

Beth Piatote

CONTENTS

INTRODUCTION

This year's *Best Debut Short Stories*, like all previous editions, is a celebration—of writers and their first-ever-published stories, of the magazine and journal editors who uplift debut voices, and of the judges who read the nominations with enthusiasm and care. This edition also celebrates the fifth anniversary of the anthology, and of the PEN/Robert J. Dau Short Story Prize for Emerging Writers.

Half a decade in, the community around the series feels both established and dynamic. The list of journals that submitted stories include familiar favorites along with new names. We've continued to refine our eligibility criteria and judging process, as we, the literary awards team at PEN America, and our prize donor, Fernanda Dau Fisher, reflect on how to define "debut" and consider what kinds of stories best represent the spirit of the prize. We have a beautiful new cover design, a collaboration between Catapult's creative director, Nicole Caputo, and Catapult magazine's in-house illustrator, Sirin Thada. After years of vital involvement with the project, we've officially added Sarah Lyn Rogers as a coeditor. And we're always proud to see previous winners cheering one another on as they publish more stories and first books.

Most years, at our annual launch reading, we have the chance to meet in person with the winning writers, judges, editors, and the PEN America team who help make all of this possible. It's a moment that seems to crystallize the idea of the anthology as a writing community. Like everyone over the past year-plus, we've had to make adjustments, including hosting our 2020 launch over Zoom. This was in many ways a welcome change, as we could include writers who were not based in or near New York City; plus the excited chats that came in over Zoom from far-flung family members were heartening—culminating in an evening that felt like real connection after so much isolation.

That's the thing about being a writer. You work in isolation to make something you hope will spark some connection with another person. Maybe your first connection is with a trusted friend who serves as a first reader, or with a teacher in a writing class. Maybe it's actually with an editor who wants to share your story with the world. That's when the connection can become exponential, when dozens or hundreds or thousands of readers suddenly have access to a crafted thing made, if not in secret, at least in private. Then it's back to seclusion to be able to make something new.

It's not usually possible to find out what made a reader connect with your work. This anthology offers a rare exception through the introductory notes from editors, whose tastes and interests can often seem opaque to writers. Our hope is that these notes are instructive and encouraging to those who pick up the anthology each year.

This year, we were also delighted to gather for an informal virtual recap with judges Nana Kwame Adjei-Brenyah, Kali Fajardo-Anstine, and Beth Piatote. They told us how much they admired the winning stories for being *unabashedly themselves*—whether that means a 900-word single sentence like Lindsay Ferguson's "Good Girls," or Qianze Zhang's "Mandy's Mary Sue," which brings us into the universe a young anime fan builds for herself from the pixels of a computer screen. Writers often contend with that question: Can I filter out other people's expectations of what a "good

story" looks or sounds like? Should I? Fajardo-Anstine spoke of
the importance of writing that has a compassionate imagination—
something that extends from your unique *unabashedly you* perspective to invite other people in. "The First Time I Said It" by
Isaac Hughes Green, "The Math of Living" by Nishanth Injam,
and "The Strong-Strong Winds" by Mathapelo Mofokeng are particularly apt examples of this ethos; each takes the singular form
it needs to allow us to live an experience—on a basketball court,
inside an eight-thousand-mile commute between two homes, in a
hot and wind-battered cemetery—alongside its characters.

While the anthology shies away from any unifying theme or
style, Adjei-Brenyah noted that a feeling of liminality comes
through in many of the pieces. "Transit" by Khaddafina Mbabazi
takes place at an airport gate; "Taxi" by Pardeep Toor drops us
into a cab ride. There is a different kind of liminality in "Maria" by
Amy Haejung and "Re: Frankie" by Mackenzie McGee: the worlds
in these stories are left just indeterminate enough to leave room on
the page for complex feelings and combinations of feelings. Piatote
suggested that short stories, more than any other form, enable the
proliferation of narratives—they are uniquely suited to convey-
ing new and untold experiences into literature. This is evident in
Alberto Reyes Morgan's "Salt," which evokes the sweat of a summer futbol game beside the dryness of the Salton Sea; in Stanley
Patrick Stocker's "The List," which speaks into unspeakable loss;
and in Heather Aruffo's "Force, Mass, Acceleration," which gives
voice to a daughter whose story has been overshadowed by her war
criminal father.

The judges also remarked on what it means to bring these stories into one anthology. As compelling as they are individually, it's
when they are placed together that they become a showcase of the

infinite things short fiction can do. And the magazines that brought us these twelve debuts have radically distinct perspectives; each represents a path in. As Adjei-Brenyah said, this book is a reminder of the many different ways a writer can "arrive."

We hope the sense of possibility extends beyond the stories and writers collected here. Fajardo-Anstine, for her part, remembered receiving hundreds of rejections before her first publication, hoping that she might be making an impression on an editor, that one might remember her name. She wants all the nominated writers to know that she *will* remember names—and that, in time, they will find their way in. Finally, though it is a joy to stop and honor each of these specific stories, it seems important to note that they are all part of a longer process: of returning again and again to the desk and to the blank page. Piatote put it this way: "Rejection and acceptance matter less when you just know there's going to be more. It's going to rain again." There are more stories coming, for all of us.

YUKA IGARASHI

SARAH LYN ROGERS

Series Editors

BEST DEBUT SHORT STORIES 2021

EDITOR'S NOTE

Is there such a thing as love at first sight? I think when it came to Lindsay Ferguson's "Good Girls" that's how it was for me. I fell in love with this piece the first time I read it. The *Barrelhouse* Love Issue was an attempt to explore love through the complex and enduring lens of Black womxn. "Good Girls" represented the multifaceted ways in which Black womxn show and receive love. From the beginning, the narrator is immediately concerned for Claudia; but what at first seems to be empathy for a friend shifts into romantic love in the end, and so we get the entire spectrum of care.

This beautifully queer story engages with the ways that Black womxn are encouraged, through familial admonishments given out of love and concern, to disassociate from our bodies and our desires. It is all a cycle. "Good Girls" gives us history, gives us depth, and shows the truth of the interior lives and interrelationships of Black womxn—in less than one thousand words. I am proud that I played even a small part in getting Lindsay's voice and talent out there to the world. If this is what we get for her very first published story, then, goodness, watch out!

Tyrese Coleman, Guest Editor
Barrelhouse

GOOD GIRLS

Lindsay Ferguson

WE'RE ON A smoke break when Claudia tells me that her husband said she's ugly when she cries, and I almost ask her, *What he do, what happened this time*, but then I think, *Don't be a fool, this is what you been waiting for*, and I take her hands, look into her eyes, and start to give her all my best ideas on how to leave Greg—Greg who treats Claudia like a greasy rag he can pull out of his back pocket whenever there's a mess, Greg who likes that Claudia's ass is wide but not her nose or her waist—and it feels good to feed her these pieces I've been carrying in the space underneath my tongue for so long, some so bitter I thought I might choke on them, and I know she doesn't really want to hear it but I tell her anyway, and I say things like *Bleach everything in his closet, yeah even his new shoes, especially those* and *Throw all his shit out the window and watch it smash real ugly to the ground*, and I can tell she doesn't mean to but she finally starts to smile, her lips full and pretty as a plum, and there under the honey glow of the streetlamp I think about how Claudia has the most beautiful brown skin I've ever seen, like Aunt Rikki, who was still beautiful even when she shaved off all her hair, piles and piles of inky black kinks on my grand- mama's kitchen floor, Aunt Rikki who spit out a mouthful of bright red venom on cream-colored tiles when Grandaddy sent her out the

3

door with a busted lip, warned her not to bring her dyke friends
around me and my cousins, not good girls like us, and I think
about how I still can't forget that day, more than forty years later,
and how I still can't forget that morning, two months ago, when
Claudia showed up for our shift with a dark purple bruise blooming at the base of her throat, how the college girls who worked
with us teased her about her hickey, and how Claudia, only a few
years older, laughed and let them believe it, and I remember how
she wouldn't meet my eyes but still asked to stay with me, how she
said no, she wasn't scared, but that she needed to teach Greg a les-
son, and that night, sitting on my couch, dinner plates resting on
our knees, everything felt right without me even trying, and I liked
that Claudia didn't ask me if I ever been married or had kids or why
there weren't any pictures of my family, and that she only wanted to
talk about the kind of TV shows I watched and the things I used to
like when I was young, and I remember how later, something deep
inside of her burst that I couldn't see, and I held Claudia as the sun
went down, the last of its glow pouring over us, an animal kind of
wail rattling from her throat and filling the space, and how I knew I
shouldn't ask but I had to know if she was like my aunt Rikki, if she
was like me, and how she said she wasn't sure but that she liked the
idea of me and my golden apartment being home, and I think about
how I believed her, even though nothing else happened that night,
even though she left before I woke the next morning and we never
talked about that moment on the couch again, and I think about
how I still believe Claudia now, as I hold her hands, and I know I
was right to find some small piece of her to touch because she leans
in and kisses me and it's the most glorious thing I've ever felt, the
sting of her lips and that hot blooming down below and of course
this is why my grandmama told me not to linger too long there

with the washcloth when I was old enough to start taking baths on my own, and I almost laugh at the memory, at the thought that she would deny me the pleasure of knowing my own body, but then Claudia is pulling away, and I'm searching for those soft brown eyes in the shadows as she says something about forgiveness and then something else about babies, but most important vows and how she can never break those, not even for a good friend like me, not even if I take her out for breakfast every Sunday or learn all the words to her favorite songs or tell her that she's beautiful when she's really not, and then I'm watching Claudia stub out the cigarette with the bottom of her shoe, watching her round the corner of the alley as she smooths the back of that stupid pink uniform that they make us wear, even though it stains like hell, even when we scrub and scrub and scrub at the grease until our fingers are white and raw, even when we know that some things, once they're set deep enough, can never be washed away.

Lindsay Ferguson lives and writes in Columbus, Ohio, where she was born and raised. When she's not helping organizations wrangle their communications, she writes fiction and paints. Her first piece of fiction, published in *Barrelhouse* and featured here, was also nominated for a 2021 Pushcart Prize.

EDITORS' NOTE

We selected this story because the language is gloriously alive and precise, playful and humorous and elegiac all at once. It reminds us that memory is speculative, that chronology and linearity are constantly shifting, that loss can loom and shine. It's both cosmic and deeply intimate, showing us the simultaneous transience and permanence of relationships. Though the story centers around a disappearance, and loss on a grand scale, it also shows us the ways the narrator and M drift and converge across time and space, the way we form a sense of self and how it blurs, and how memory becomes myth. It is imaginative and innovative with both language and form. With a surrealism that feels real and intimate, this writer is attuned to the subtleties and nuances of the people and relationships that our lives orbit around, that illuminate and change the course of our lives, that we speculate about but ultimately cannot know.

Combining scientific fact, dreams, theory, and observant vignettes, every assured sentence of this story has the weight and rhythm of poetry. It moved us the moment we read it. It's the kind of story that we wanted to reread and reread, each time discovering a new facet of it. We knew that this writer's voice was singular and expansive.

Rose Skelton, Fiction Editor
K-Ming Chang, Assistant Fiction Editor
Waxwing Literary Journal

MARIA

Amy Haejung

THE NEXT DAY the news headlines were all about the moon: theories about its disappearance, scientific fumbling and weird conspiracies and wild speculation. Some people said the moon was tired of looking at us for so many millennia, unable to turn away, tidally locked in a stare to the death, and had finally freed itself. Some said the United States and North Korea had accidentally disintegrated it in competing nuclear explosions. Others said aliens.

There was live coverage, breaking news headlines, constant updates for a week and a half, until it became clear that the moon was indeed gone, not merely hidden by some illusive celestial mechanism, and that it wasn't likely to come back anytime soon or by any human means. Then came the longform essays and thought pieces, hot takes and even eulogies, with titles like "What Does the Moon Mean to Us Now That It's Gone?" and "In Memoriam: The Illustrated Life of the Moon."

Then the news cycle moved on, and nobody talked about the moon anymore, everyone seemed to forget it had ever hung pearly in our sky, a shiny earring, blank and bright.

LONG BEFORE THE moon's disappearance, M and I started a Sailor Moon club. At first it was just the two of us, and we aggressively protected our monogamy, communing only through ear-whispers and denying membership to dozens of tearful classmates. They didn't even know what Sailor Moon was, just resented, with the transparency of childhood, the phonic finality of the word *no*. But our homeroom teacher told us we were Leaving People Out and sent us to peer mediation, which meant that we spent an entire recess and math period seated at a circular table across from two fifth graders and the guidance counselor, mushing our elbows into the cool white laminate and attempting to chew our soggy peanut-butter-and-jelly sandwiches somewhat attentively. Finally we agreed to open our club to the public, but the next week we were back in peer mediation; I'd been watching WWE with my brother, and we'd turned the club into an Ultimate Sailor Fight to the Death, making all the white girls fight each other for the titles of Sailor Mercury, Venus, Mars, and Jupiter.

M and I became friends because we were the only two Asians in our grade. I don't remember much of my playground life before our convergence, just that I spent every recess circling a sliding pole alone, tethering myself to it with one hand and letting the rest of my body fall away, on the cusp of collapse. One coldly sunny day a beautiful black-haired girl joined my solitary orbit in silence, which she finally broke to compliment my Velcro Mulan sneakers. This, of course, was M.

The next Saturday my mom and I stood outside her front door, and a woman with short blond hair and a raised mole near her bottom lip let us in. I thought we had the wrong house, but M came running down the stairs, and we went down to the basement while our moms sat at the kitchen counter chatting in those plasticky voices. After we made brownies in her Easy-Bake Oven, she told me her Korean name meant *precious pearl*. I was so envious I asked my grandmother what my name meant, pressing her until she said *beautiful, pure, perfect*.

WITH THE MOON'S absence, the nights became deeper and the stars multiplied like shining maggots, shivering and wet, a whole net of them strung across the sky. They looked so near, almost ready to drizzle down, wobbling like droplets barely clinging to the rim of an umbrella. Then safe night driving won out over star-gazing as a public concern, and the government passed new laws mandating streetlights at intervals commensurate with population density. After that, the night skies were lighter and emptier than ever.

My grandmother joked that she wouldn't have to give us money on Lunar New Year anymore. None of the children's hanboks she'd brought years ago from Korea fit us anyway, and it felt weird to do the formal bow in regular clothes, as if we were performing out of costume. She said Koreans used to believe there were fire dogs that chased the sun and moon, and maybe one finally got the moon, which didn't seem less reasonable than any of the other hypotheses.

In the end the festivities proceeded essentially as usual, the lunar part in name only, an empty signifier. The moon so easily became a thing of myth I couldn't help wondering if that was all it had ever been.

———

TEACHERS WOULD ALWAYS mix up our names. Even some class-mates did, and at first M and I would smile proudly, considering sameness and interchangeability evidence of our deep intimacy, a private conspiracy. We used to look into each other like mirrors, matching ourselves to our reflections. But by fourth grade, we had caught Individualism. We both wanted to be Original, and constantly accused each other of Copying. I was furious when her mom bought her the same skirts as me, and she said I only auditioned for the school play because she had. I started ballet in secret, because I didn't want her to know I was Copying, and took art lessons in secret, because I didn't want her to Copy.

And so our lives became more and more hidden from each other, until she transferred schools in seventh grade, and I realized we were no longer friends.

THE TIDES SHRUNK, flattened themselves back against the ocean bed, no longer impelled by lunar gravity to resist the pull of the earth's core. Sometimes the ocean looked almost as flat and smooth as a cut of jade, seemingly solid until something dropped into it and sunk, stonelike.

The stock market went haywire; tourism to popular surfing des-tinations plummeted. Billabong and Quiksilver almost went out of business, then decided to partner with inland surf parks and became more lucrative than ever. They said these artificial pools had better, more consistent waves than the ocean ever had, which wasn't false. Soon these pools proliferated and became as famil-iar as ice skating rinks. Landlocked states like Arizona and Utah boasted the biggest parks and became the new surfing hubs, while Hawaii and California clung feebly to the aesthetic.

I went to college in a state named after the ocean, but I never saw it when I was there. I started with a major in environmental science and a concentration in post-lunar studies, riding a surge of speculative interest in the natural world. Everyone was talking about a total reorganization of nature, mass extinctions and a new order of animals, a shift in the earth's axis and accelerated climate change, spiritual and astrological implications. When it became evident none of these changes would occur for many human life-times, the intellectual frenzy dwindled, and then astronomy and environmental science were about as popular as they'd been before. Astrology, however, continued to gain devotees.

I SAW HER one last time at the state fair, where I'd gone that high school summer with the latest of a rotating cast of friends. We were waiting in line for the Wave Swinger, that aerial carousel-sibling that flung its suspended seats in a circuit.

We were watching all these people in controlled flight, and then I picked out a face among the others. A pale yellow face, cradled by the blackest hair I'd never seen again after elementary school. Small doll-like features frozen in an open-mouthed smile, the expression somehow empty, an empty house with all the windows open, the air rushing through. Slowly she descended, spiraling slower and lower, until she slid out of the seat and alighted on the ground, and gravity returned to her—her ruffled white dress spilling out of the chair, the mass of her hair settling like a large bird folding its wings.

She started walking briskly to the exit, and I rushed through the entrance gate, shouted her name—it was such a common name, but she was the first person I knew with it, and it had sounded so graceful, exalted. I never knew anyone with her name intimately after that; they all seemed so unrelentingly ordinary, and perhaps I'd wanted to preserve a kind of sanctity. She turned, scanned past me, then came back to my face, and for a moment we were alone, looking at each other looking at each other.

But then over the speakers the ride operator said *Everyone please be seated*, and I saw that I was one of the last unseated stragglers. She shrugged, smiled, and waved. I moved toward my precarious chair of choice, and she turned away.

In midair I thought about that painted smile, looked for a flash of white among the dotted crowds. While my friends and I waited in line for funnel cake and deep-fried Oreos, my eyes kept searching, straying like a recalibrating compass needle. By nighttime, I had walked through the entire fair looking for her, but she was gone.

And then the moon disappeared.

IN MY HISTORY of Lunar Studies core lecture, which was more humanities than science, the professor projected a huge, high-definition photograph of the moon, its parts labeled like an anatomical diagram, each dark crater and mare named—they were called maria, Latin for *seas*, because astronomers once thought they were lunar lakes, promising life. They turned out to be basaltic scars from eons-old volcanic eruptions, but the misnomers remained: Mare Nubium, sea of clouds; Mare Serenitatis, sea of serenity; Mare Cognitum, sea that has become known. And so on.

The professor began, *They say the moon and the earth were once one body, until a collision with another planet punched a hole in the earth. What we lost accreted in the form of the moon, faithful satellite, phantom limb.*

The students *mmmmmm*-ed deeply. I decided to transfer to the English department.

THE FULL MOON was doubled in the ocean, we were kids again in the sand and M was counting seashells, and then we were at her house, but it didn't look anything like the one I remembered. Everything was ancient and wooded and dark, and the moonlight spilled through the open windows, draping us in a silvery gauze.

I turned to her again and she was an adult, and I was, too. She said she wanted to cut her hair, which I saw was so long it pooled around her feet. I picked up a pair of scissors and began to cut it, shorter and shorter, sheets of black falling to the floor, and then when she spun around I saw my own face.

MAYBE THE MOON didn't really disappear, and maybe M didn't either. Maybe she's in San Diego with a husband and kids, honeyed from the sun, selling handmade jewelry and teaching at a yoga studio. Maybe I accepted her Facebook friend request, but neither of us sent the first message. But would any of that change anything? This isn't about anyone except her, the version of her that lived between my brain and my skull, grew into my mind.

The face in the mirror smiles when I smile. Does it matter whose face it is?

———————————

Amy Haejung lives in New York and works as a freelance copy editor and proofreader. She is a 2021 Kweli Emerging Writer Fellow and was a finalist for the 2020 Kundiman Mentorship Lab in fiction.

EDITOR'S NOTE

Khaddafina Mbabazi's story "Transit" was a pleasure to read, the work of an author with clearly formidable skill. Her well-developed characters and carefully paced plot lead the reader through a suspenseful and dynamic tale. We were impressed with the story's ability to launch a strong social critique without ever becoming didactic. We believed our readers, too, would be engrossed by Mbabazi's story.

Allison Wright, Publisher and Executive Editor
Virginia Quarterly Review

TRANSIT

Khaddafina Mbabazi

AT HEATHROW, THREE hours before her flight to Boston, Thandi
was in one of the shower rooms below the Galleries lounge in
Terminal 5. A previous tenant—someone who, at some point in the
day, had been in there before her, before every inch of the shower
room was cleaned, its towels and various amenities replaced—had
left a trace of themselves: the radio on, the dial turned to Classic
FM. Which meant that Thandi had spent the last twenty minutes
listening to Fauré and Vaughan Williams. Now it was Handel.
From Solomon: "The Arrival of the Queen of Sheba."

This was the first part of her transit routine, her routine between flights. After bathing and dressing, she'd go downstairs to
do her usual walkabout, grazing the possibilities of the duty-free
floor—perfume, whiskey, rare chocolates, the sort that were rare
in Nairobi. Then she would find a place to eat. If she was with
her husband, Kimani—who liked what he liked and disliked what
he disliked, which in the case of airports was the buzz and bustle
of the duty-free floor—she'd return to the lounge and dine with
him there. But if she was traveling alone, she could play with time.
Reverse the order of things. Could, for instance, sample one of the
terminal's restaurants. Three months ago, the last time she was here
at Heathrow (en route to Greece for a Nigerian friend's wedding),

17

she'd dined at one of the newer places. It was called Pardee (in Middle English: "by God"), a place where they served meals that were elegant and shrapnel-small: the newest tentacle of Terminal 5's desire to be a transient playhouse of Great British luxury.

She wasn't hungry now. And as she left the shower room and ascended the stairs to the second level, where the lounge was, she was thinking that she just wanted to be in her corner, a newspaper in one hand, a glass of red wine in the other. Before going off to shower, she'd marked the spot as hers. Left her blazer on the back of the chair and a newspaper on the small round table headline-up ("May's Brexit Deal Crushed by Commons").

This was where she always sat. Right by the big panels of windows through which one could spy the glidings of aircraft and next to a host of beautiful and curious things: pots of white lilacs; other pots containing flowers that looked like wheat; the cool Heathrow light that pressed its soft hand in; the life-sized statues of several horses: Black and sinewed, tails swept to the right of their bodies. Focused. Unmoving. Like sentries standing guard.

She was surprised—shocked, to be precise—to find that her spot had been taken, annexed by a woman who was drinking tea and eating shortbread biscuits. The woman had folded Thandi's newspaper and pushed it away so that one half was dangling off the side of the table and the other was being used as a tray.

Thandi, standing now behind the woman, tugged at the blazer and said, "Excuse me."

The woman turned around slowly, unsurely, as though steeling herself to encounter something wild, then she launched her body off the chair and said, "Oh god. Did I take your place?"

The thief had the voice of a smoker. The yellowed teeth of one too. Thandi, who'd grabbed her blazer off the back of the chair as the woman stretched around, tossed her things onto the sofa behind them. Anyone watching would likely deduce that a dramatic affair was about to take place. The thought had crossed her mind, but it embarrassed Thandi—average of height, soft-bodied, tastefully modest in her beige attire of cigarette trousers and cashmere knit; a woman, these days, who prided herself on being well behaved. Neutral.

"I didn't realize that someone was sitting here. Honestly. I'm a very absent-minded person. I'm so sorry," said the woman.

"It's fine," Thandi said.

"No. You were here first. I'll move." The woman picked up her tea and biscuits and set them down on the square table by the sofa. Then she sat next to Thandi's recaptured things. "It's yours now," she announced. "I have vacated your territory."

"You didn't have to do that," Thandi said, sounding perfectly unoffended.

"Well, I'm not going back. So if you change your mind . . ." The woman laughed—a deep barbecued sound. Then she extended her hand and said, "I'm Flannery."

She was tall, this Flannery. Blond, loose-skinned, astonishingly white. She wore a flowered top with long sleeves, a knee-length skirt, and slip-ons on her feet—an outfit that Thandi noted disapprovingly. But she accepted the hand nonetheless, shook it, and said, "I'm Thandiwe."

"My god, you're pretty, aren't you?" Flannery said. "And what a wonderful name!"

"Thanks. Yours too." Thandi truly felt this way. That a name like Flannery was noteworthy. But she imagined it had sounded insincere.

"Where is it from?" Flannery asked.

"Southern Africa somewhere."

"Wonderful." Flannery smiled. Said, "I used to have a friend from South Africa. Lovely girl. Itha Swanepoel. But I don't think you'd know her, would you?" She paused, narrowing gray eyes at Thandi.

"Sorry. No. I don't know any Ithas."

"Of course. She'd be my age now. Which is old." Flannery laughed.

"I'm from Uganda. We don't have Ithas or Swanepoels," Thandi said.

Flannery furrowed her brow. "Oh," she said. Her voice dropped and she sounded disappointed when she said, "Well, I'm sorry. I don't know anyone from Uganda. Although I guess now I do."

Flannery—who'd been flipping through pages of *The Mail on Sunday*—returned to her reading. And Thandi thought how bizarre that exchange had been, though she couldn't say why it was bizarre, only that it was. Kimani, the more articulate of the two, more quickly discerning, would've been able to pin it down. She pulled out her phone to text him, but just at that moment Flannery looked up and said, "Uganda? Is that the one where the president was a cannibal? Long ago, I mean, not now. Gosh, I should hope not now!"

"Rumored, yes. But I doubt it."

"I can't even begin to imagine it!"

The women laughed, regarding each other like two unacquainted animals, each sniffing the other out, Flannery expecting a response, Thandi denying her one, the moment finally scattered by an announcement from the front desk: *Mr. Vikram Rao? Mr. Vikram Rao, could you make yourself known to a member of staff, please.*

EIGHTEEN YEARS AGO, when Thandi was still new to travel, when she left Uganda for the first time—an unripened twenty-year-old accompanying her father, both of them laughably clothed for the Cape Town winter—airports made her anxious. Made her want to heave. This was a story that the Thandi of that time told often enough that it had become a shibboleth of her life. But it was not fully true. The problem wasn't the airports themselves. Not really. Not on their own. Actually, her anxiety about travel had been activated long before she set foot in an airport. Before actual travel. As she stood in well-aired but penitential embassy rooms, providing answers to irksome questions: Do you have family here? In Uganda? ("Yes," she'd say, "my parents. Two sisters and two brothers.") Any close family ties? (And Thandi would wonder if Europeans and Americans had different definitions of "close family." For what could be closer than your own blood?) A husband, for example? Children? ("Oh, no. I'm not ready for that," Thandi would proclaim, laughing, misunderstanding the question to be one of mere curiosity.) Time and again, for several years, her visa applications were denied.

A year after her Cape Town trip, she'd graduated from Makerere with a degree in development studies and began working at a development agency in Kampala. It was run by a mix of white people: a Frenchman, an American from Maine, and a Rhodesian woman— the Uganda expert, as they called her—who'd lived in Kampala for a year. As a new recruit, Thandi was to be trained in America, so she spent a month in New York in July—her first time out of Africa. After three years at the agency, she achieved something unheard of for the locals and became a fairly prominent figure in the organization. Together with the Rhodesian, she was invited to a big international development conference in London—a sign of her growing currency.

At the British embassy (in the interview room), the interviewer had asked the same genus of questions. This was enough to annoy Thandi but not to alarm her. After all, he'd asked the same of the Rhodesian, and by then Thandi had been to America and returned and had the visa and stamps to prove it. But the same man, two weeks later, signed his initials to the bottom of a letter declaring that her application for a visa to the United Kingdom had been denied. He was not convinced, he wrote, that she had close enough family ties to her home country. The Rhodesian, with her green Zimbabwean passport, did not suffer the same fate.

Thandi appealed the decision on the basis that the interviewer's fixation on her family ties (i.e., her marital status) was sexist and that she'd recently returned from a trip to America, evidence that she had no migratory intent. If I could leave America, Thandi wrote, the greatest country on earth, and return home to Uganda, the Pearl of Africa itself, why would I elect to remain in Britain—a country that looks at the shadow of its empire and does not yet recognize it as a shadow at all? That elegant savagery (which in the end was the death knell of Thandi's appeal) belonged to her father, Robert: a university professor who did not believe that any country was great, let alone greatest; who was in fact convinced that America was an appalling force in the world; who had long ago stopped traveling outside of Africa; and who liked to say things like, Why should I leave Africa? I am from Africa. And from what I can tell, non-Africans don't like to bathe. Why should I, a clean man, dispatch myself to the lands of the dirty?

Even when she began to travel a little more, she wasn't able to enjoy it. Wasn't sure that the prospect of her-as-tourist had lost its repellent shimmer. She dreaded the long waits at Hamad International: the crowds, the unbearable toilets, the airport workers that tailed her in duty-free shops, afraid that she might steal a bottle of expensive lotion or a pair of high-end shoes. But it was Brussels—where they kept travelers to Africa quarantined in a faraway section of the airport—that had delivered the worst experiences.

Once, having been granted a scholarship by the Chinese government to do a master's at Shanghai Jiao Tong University, she had a twelve-hour wait in Brussels before a flight out to Pudong Airport. Surprisingly, the Belgian officials in Kampala (a nasty bunch from an even nastier country, her father had pre-warned) granted her a transit visa. But once she arrived, the officer had refused to land her. He looked down at her papers (passport, tickets, SJTU admissions letter) and then, without stamping her passport, handed them back to her. She asked him why he hadn't stamped the passport. "I need an entry stamp to go through," she said.

"Why should I let you through?" he asked. "I see no reason for you to come into Belgium. I can see you're continuing on to China later today. In a few hours in fact."

"No, not in a few hours. In half a day! It says so on my ticket, didn't you read it?"

The officer looked at her keenly through his small brown eyes. "And why should I believe that you'd come back?" he asked.

"Why shouldn't you?" she countered.

The officer regarded her for a long moment, and Thandi tried but failed to imagine what thoughts accompanied that rampant gaze.

Finally, blinking out of his silent reverie, he said, "You have an

onward flight to Pudong Airport. I suggest you walk to your terminal and wait for your flight. I'm sorry, but I cannot land you."

"But I have a valid transit visa!" Thandi protested. She had not
yet learned that immigration officers were authorities in the same
way that policemen were authorities, that they expected immediate
deference.

"And what do you plan on doing with it?"

"I am supposed to meet a friend for lunch at a place called the
Lobster House. Afterward, we will go shopping in Les Galeries
Royales Saint-Hubert and then she will drive me back to the airport." None of this was true. Those places existed, but far above
Thandi's fiscal capacity. But a week before she was due to travel,
a friend (a Murundi girl who'd lived in Belgium and now lived in
Kampala with her Muganda boyfriend) had advised her to name
real places so as to appear less suspicious. In reality, Thandi
planned to just walk around the city, get some fresh air, take some
photos of Belgian landmarks, and then find a cheap café to have
lunch at. But her friend had said the posher the itinerary, the better.
She'd even made Thandi practice the words, so that her French (a
language she'd relinquished in primary school) sounded as close to
native as possible.

The officer cocked his head to the side, as though he were exam-
ining her afresh. From a new angle. Thandi began to have the sense
that she had triumphed, but then his head lifted back up and his
shoulders started to jig up and down and she realized that he was
laughing. "I'm sorry," he said. "I cannot take the risk of landing
you. You expect me to believe that you will come back? We have
had a large number of people like you in recent years. Trying to
settle here and being less than honest about it."

"I'm not trying to settle. I just don't want to be stuck here for twelve hours! It's Shanghai Jiao Tong University! Do you think I would throw away that opportunity to stay here in Brussels? And do what exactly? Be a house girl?"

"I have never heard of this university," the man said. "And I am beginning to lose my patience."

"I have a valid transit visa!" Thandi cried and her face was astonished, her eyes welling up and her shoulders shaking with fury. "This is so bloody unfair!"

The Belgian (who was only slightly lighter than her, who Thandi deduced was probably Arab) didn't enjoy this kind of thing—women coming apart at the seams. He wagged a menacing finger at her and said, "Would you prefer that I send you back to your country? Hmm? Just be grateful that I haven't done that. I could do it very easily. Believe me. Now go to your terminal. Go. Go!" He called on the couple behind her to step forward, then looked at her one last time and made the shoo motion with his hand. Thandi obeyed.

An older Thandi, whenever she looked back on this, would cringe at this moment. The admission of impotence, the compliance with an irrational pecking order. Even now she wished it away—a reminder that she had once been weak. But of course it was too late. The moment had already pressed into the clay of her, become a part of the ceramics of who she was. By the time she boarded the plane, twelve hours later, it was a hard and permanent thing.

What was not permanent, what years of frequent travel had by now worn away, was her anxiety. Nine years ago, when success and marriage came (to William Kimani of landed Kikuyu stock), Thandi shed her old self for a new one: better clothed, better cared-for; a life propelled by the force of a Kipling decree: *Yours is the Earth and everything that's in it.* She discovered how to travel

well. How to defend herself against indignity. Now, Thandi didn't
have the kinds of struggles she'd once had. Almost always, she and
Kimani traveled in Business (and occasionally, if they were feeling indulgent, First). Ten-year visas—a thing unheard of by the old
Thandi—were bequeathed to them without fear. With ease. For
this was what the Kimanis had demanded of the world—a life un-
encumbered by inconvenience. And this was what the world had
granted.

There was a tension in this for Thandi—the kind one would
expect in a woman who was born in the midseventies into a young
and precarious middle class, one whose brilliant academic of
a father was underpaid, whose mother's pride as one of the first
African dukawallas was for decades chafed by the modest reality
of her sales. Before meeting Kimani (at Shanghai Jiao Tong) Thandi
knew, abstractly, that there were people like this. People like her
living lives of immense privilege and access. But that world had
seemed sealed off. And even though she was in it, even though the
seal had been broken open, she still sometimes felt like an inter-
loper. Not in places like these—foreign lands where no one knew
her—but at home in Karen when Kimani would speak to the children of his ancestors, a gilded tail of memory that stretched back
to touch the seventeenth century. And when the question inevitably
came—"What about your people, Mummy?"—what could she say?
She knew of her grandfathers—one a tradesman, one a lay church
preacher—and their fathers, simple Kiga peasants both. But that
was where the line ended.

OUTSIDE AS AFTERNOON waned, the light began its dying, its soft-
handed retreat. But inside the lounge, which in Thandi's mind fell

under the mediation of airport time, and which had little corre-
spondence to normal time—children zipping around at midnight,
adults getting spa treatments or conducting business over phones
at 2:00 a.m.—the day had picked up. Brought with it an invasion
of travelers. Sitting now by the pot of white lilacs, on the opposite end of Thandi and Flannery, was a family of four—a highly
Scandinavian middle-aged couple and their blond boys. Thandi's
chair—empty in the wake of Flannery's evacuation—was now occupied by a pixie-haired white woman, clad in a black hoodie and
matching joggers. And in the adjacent seat, a gentleman in a blue
Kaunda suit.

Thandi was scrolling through emails on her computer when a
loud exchange broke out at reception. It was the Vikram Rao from
before and the blue-suited woman at the front desk. The reasons
were unclear, and Thandi wouldn't have ordinarily taken heed, but
she was close enough to the entrance that she caught the end of
Mr. Rao's attack. "You people are fucking useless! And you're supposedly the ones that brought us civilization! You wonder why the
Asians and the Arabs are so far ahead of you in hospitality—and
in nearly everything else these days? This! Is! Why!" He walked
away, making for the exit, but then turned back around and continued at the receptionist: "I should have known not to use these
mildewed European airlines and airports. I should have flown out
of Abu Dhabi!" Thandi laughed at the dramatics, then returned to
her emails.

"Then why didn't you?" Flannery said, head craned back. She
turned to Thandi. "These rich people! These bloody rich people!
And they wonder why the whole world hates them." She shook her
head, face scrunched in great disgust, then, feeling the need to explain herself to Thandi, put her hands on her chest and added, "I'm

only here because I'm Silver, like most of these people, I'd assume. I tried to get an upgrade. They say if you dress nicely, you're more likely to get one. I shouldn't have believed it. One has to be rich to get even the tiniest sliver these days. Well, I am not rich. And I tell you what else? At moments like these, I'm glad not to be one of them." She pointed a finger at the empty space that Mr. Rao, only moments ago, had wrathfully occupied.

"Yes. That was unnecessary," Thandi said, though this was more for Flannery, whose fulmination had caught her off guard.

"I'm glad we're of one mind. For a moment I wondered if you were . . . you know . . . a part of that particular species. I would have told Mr. Raul right off if that was me. Why didn't she tell him off?" she inquired, palms and shoulders raised high.

"I think it was Rao," Thandi said.

"It's a matter of manners," Flannery pressed.

"Maybe we give him the benefit of the doubt. You never know in these situations." This—Thandi's sympathy offer—was met with a bruised stare. And Thandi thought, then, that she saw something move through Flannery.

Coil; then uncoil.

"Well, I suppose I can't argue with that." Flannery stood. "I'm going to get myself another cup. Do you want one?"

"Oh. Thanks. A glass of dry red would be nice."

Briefly, Thandi's gaze followed Flannery as she moved toward the bar, the hard sandals on her feet clacking loudly against the floor, the hard muscular legs which hadn't been oiled, the slow gait, slower than Thandi was used to from white people who were always, it seemed to her, in a great carnivorous rush. (Kimani's favorite edict in the middle of the busy streets of Marylebone: "Walk fast. This is London.")

When Flannery returned—without her tea, with two glasses of red instead—she said to Thandi, "So what is it you do in Uganda?"

"I'm in the dry-cleaning business," Thandi said. "But I don't live there. I live in Nairobi, where my husband is from."

"Is that where you're going?"

"No. Boston."

"What takes you to Boston? Is it work?"

"A little bit of work. But mostly pleasure."

"Ohhh, lucky you. There won't be much pleasure for me where I'm going. Lisbon. Just work work work." Flannery sipped her wine. "And will you be staying at a hotel or . . . ?"

"With friends of mine who live there." This was false. Her travel agent had booked her a top-floor room at the Mandarin, but Thandi saw no need to divulge this information.

"Doooo theyyy?" Flannery said. "What are they doing there, then?"

Thandi, who was used to this sort of thing from strangers—curiosity that churned into something more suspicious—was still not immune to its antagonizing power.

"Working. Living. Paying their taxes," she said.

"I'm sorry," Flannery said. "I didn't mean to intrude." She leaned back against the sofa, picked up her wine and a copy of OK! magazine (which Thandi knew she couldn't possibly have procured from the lounge, had to have purchased from one of the bookshops downstairs). Thandi, who suddenly recalled that she had things to do (duty-free items to collect, food to eat so as to avoid airplane food), stood and announced her intention to leave.

"But the flight doesn't leave for another two hours. Are you going to lug that thing around? For two hours? Why don't you leave it here?" She pointed at Thandi's carry-on. "I'll watch over it for you since my flight leaves later than yours." And something must've alighted on Thandi's face, because Flannery added, "You don't think I'd steal anything, do you?"

"I don't know you," Thandi said.

"It's up to you." Flannery shrugged, returning to her copy of *OK!* "All I'm doing is offering."

Thandi could not explain, then, the sensation that came over her: an emulsion of dread and pity. She took a moment to appraise this Flannery, thinking she was tiresome, imagining how she must flounder in her day-to-day, bumping along winds of self-harm, unable not to warp her human interactions. Much like a gnat. But harmless, Thandi concluded. And anyway an act of theft in this place of white lilacs and black horses seemed unlikely to her.

Thandi acquiesced. "Okay. I'll be back in an hour. Thanks."

FLANNERY WAITED TILL 6:17. It seemed like a good sign, the fifteen minutes that Thandi had been away. She walked over to the woman who occupied her former seat, the chair from which she'd been evicted, and tapped her on the shoulder. The woman turned around, her face unable to feign interest.

"Could I ask of you a favor?" Flannery said.

"Yes?"

"I'm just going to pop over to the bathroom. Would you watch my things while I'm gone? I'm sitting over there." She pointed to the leather sofa, her magazines and large duty-free bag.

"Okay, but I'm leaving in five minutes. I won't be responsible for your things after."

Flannery nodded in thanks. She searched for the ladies' bathroom, Thandi's suitcase in tow, and when she found it—a place of gleaming dark walls and elegant vanity tops—ensconced herself in a large stall.

The carry-on itself was not quite what she'd imagined: hard, black, and unfussy. But she stuck to her plan, still. Emptied it, one by one, of its contents. The small silver computer, the transparent bag with creams and cosmetics, the blue jeans, the cotton underwear, the newspapers, these ubiquitous things were of no interest to her. Nor, in the end, was the scarf—its square white center exploding with brown bird plumes. These things were, some of them, curious. But they did not count as evidence.

This fact satisfied Flannery. She repacked the case, everything in order, and after emptying her bladder, pulled up the carry-on's handle and wheeled it out of the stall. She stood before the mirror, washing her hands, gazing at her blue-veined face, feeling the split-second sadness to which she'd lately grown accustomed when she looked in a mirror, and the understanding that came with it: that she could no longer be counted among the beautiful. Not at fifty-four.

Flannery recalled that she'd been beautiful once. That she'd been beautiful in Lichfield—where she was from—and that there was a time when hers would have bested the beauty of the Thandis of the world. She thought of all the poor young girls in Lichfield growing up now, neighbors of other young girls, the kind who didn't exist in Lichfield forty years ago. How unfortunate that they were born in this fragile age, one where every Thandi expected to be accommodated and indulged at the expense of others.

She dried her hands with a white face towel, which she gathered (disapprovingly) that she was meant to add to the growing tower under the sink. She was nearly dismayed to find that the bottle of hand lotion was empty, until she recalled Thandi's bag of creams. Flannery unzipped the case and pulled the bag out for close examination.

They were the first things she saw when she lifted the bag to eye level: small and skull-white, gleaming at her with menace, as though they'd been biding their time, waiting all along to be discovered—these pots of diamond-infused face creams.

BY THE TIME Thandi reemerged from below—with her own duty-free bag (wine for her Boston friends, chocolates for their children), the gate to her flight had opened. She saw her carry-on, pulled right up against Flannery, who was asleep, stretched out on the sofa, sandals off, arms folded over her belly. She stood over her for a moment, hesitant, trying to decide whether to wake her. To say thank you and goodbye. But then Flannery exhaled deeply, rolled onto her left side, and turned her back to Thandi, who took this as a signal to leave.

On her way out, the lady at the front desk (the same one who'd been at the receiving end of Vikram Rao's rebuke) said that they weren't boarding premium passengers yet. "We'll let you know. You can still relax, Mrs. Kimani," she said. But it would feel awkward going back, and anyway Thandi preferred to be early as opposed to on time. She thought about Flannery as she made her way down to the gate. She'd found it alarming at first, how her carry-on handle, which she'd left folded down, stood lifted like an antenna, but then she imagined that Flannery had pulled it up to wheel the bag closer. In the end, she decided, she'd had the right idea about the woman. And the more that she thought about it, what did it matter if Flannery had taken something? Everything she required—passport, wallet, jewelry—stayed with her at all times, hedged in a tight grasp between arm and rib. The rest was easily substituted.

At the gate, where there was a steady swell of passengers, Thandi was first in a line of five. On the other side of the barrier, a gate agent—short and red-haired, the name Stephen etched onto a badge—was flanked by two men. Stephen regarded her and said, "Step forward, madam." Thandi, who was reading phone messages in her left hand, gave the man her passport and boarding pass with her right. So she didn't see it, that moment when he turned to the men behind him. But she heard it. Heard the whispered baritone of "This is her." Thandi looked up, with sudden force, at men who appeared to be scrutinizing her. Then she looked behind her and around her at the assembly of travelers, to try to locate the suspicious one among them. By the time she turned around, the two men—average of height and slim as reeds (and who knew that slimness could be so menacing!)—had moved past the barrier to enclose her.

"Will you follow us please, ma'am?" the one with no beard said. He pointed at her carry-on. "I'll take that," he added. She relinquished it without pause. But when the other man, the one on her left, pointed to her bag and said, "That, too," she refused.

"No," Thandi said. But he picked it out of her hands easily, as though he were confiscating something from a small child.

Thandi walked behind one and in front of the other and replayed the sound of that *no* in her mind. This was a habit that followed precarious moments, when she felt unsure of whatever had just found its way out of her mouth. Sometimes, the words in her head disappeared as though carried off by some interior wind. But now all she could think about was that *no*: that a weaker *no*, a more faltering *no*, had probably never been uttered by a Kimani. She wanted to cry out, to curse, though she couldn't imagine what she'd say if she did. And of course she knew, without having to look (though she stole a dismayed glance before she stepped into the lift), that the assembly of people she'd turned to before had now turned to her. Were watching her. Kneading her into various ill-made shapes.

SOMEWHERE DEEP INSIDE the belly of Heathrow Airport—somewhere that was the kind of place she'd heard of but had not had to imagine—Thandi sat. The room was void of extravagance or care. There were two red chairs on either end of a white table, a boxy telephone attached to the wall, and a black box—an audio recorder. On her way in, they'd passed others like it and she saw a tall man wearing a khamis exiting the room that neighbored hers.

An hour passed and she wondered what on earth the men were doing, though through the window she could see the arm of the one that guarded the door. The other, the one who'd spoken first and who she now saw was the leader between them and who she was now sure would be conducting some kind of interrogation, had wandered out of view.

Thandi had had some time to brood. To consider the kinds of things that Kimani would think of: protocols, legality, their London lawyers. She remembered them now because she was convinced that the officers—or whatever they were—had not behaved properly or followed the right protocols. She intended, when they brought her things back in, to phone her lawyers right away and prepare them to do ferocious battle. But in the meantime her mind

kept wandering off to the passengers on the plane. And she cringed
at the thought of how she must have caused them a delay. Wondered
if at this moment, a flight attendant was announcing her name to
everyone on board: this is the final boarding call for passenger
Thandiwe Kimani. And whether the other travelers would put two
and two together, would identify her as the suspicious figure that
had been whisked away. Thandi wondered if a few of them would
google her, and what they'd make of their findings: a recent *Forbes*
list, interviews with one or two of the loud Kimanis (second cousins
of her husband), speculation about how many square miles of land
they owned. Perhaps they would even come across an article in a
British tabloid from two years ago, the infamous one that existed,
now, as mere screenshots: "These Black Africans Are Crazy Rich.
But Where Does Their Money Come From?"

By the time the door cracked open, bringing with it the two officers, Thandi had been waiting for two hours. She was sure she'd
missed her flight. She was fuming.

The beardless man sat down across from her. And she saw her
captor properly then—the pale pear of his face, the brown hair
that was overmoist, the smallness of his mouth, which, when he
talked, when he said, "Kee-MA-nny, is that how you say it?" barely
moved—and was struck by how weak he looked.

She allowed herself to imagine that he was more easily overcome
than she'd first thought.

The officers got on with their duties in the order they'd explained, but this was after informing her that they had the right to
do whatever they were about to do under the law, and that if she
resisted, at best they would keep her in the room for as long as they
desired, and at worst they would lock her up in a cell.

Thandi, who'd refused to open her bags when they asked, who had said, "If you want to open it, you open it. You're the one that brought me here," sat in silence. She eyed the men intensely, as they searched her bags and swabbed them. She did not waver, even in those moments when they glanced up from their rifling and caught her eye. She wanted to convey something: that she, too, was watching them and had marked them. The search and swab took ten minutes, and then the officer, the pale one, announced that they were done. "I'll be back with the results. In the meantime, pack this all up," he said. He collected his swabs and made for the door, but then turned back, picked up her bag of creams, and said, "I'll be taking this."

THEY RELEASED HER, eventually, once it was ascertained that she was carrying nothing prohibited. Once it had become clear that they had gotten something terribly wrong. But not before reporting these facts to her without apology. Informing her that they were simply doing their duties, that they had done nothing wrong, they hoped she understood that, and that it wasn't their policy to reimburse passengers for missed flights.

Thandi—who by then had informed the lawyers of the situation, two big-time barristers who were presently en route to Heathrow—stood to pack her things. She couldn't be sure exactly when it had happened, but something old and hard had broken inside of her. The officers watched her as she put her handbag on her shoulder and lifted the carry-on handle.

"I'm free to go?" she asked. They nodded, yes.

Thandi walked out of the detention room and passed the officer who was holding the door open. She ambled a few feet forward, then turned around and said to him, "Do you have children?"

The officer frowned, indicating that the question was odd and that he had no more time in his day to give her, but still he said, "Yes."

And then Thandi spat on the floor. "You are nothing!" she said to him.

He looked up, face even whiter than before, and said, "I'm sorry?"

"I said you're nothing! Just a fucking worker! And your children will be nothing and their children too. Never forget that."

It would take Thandi some time to connect the cardinal dots of her detention. Three weeks, to be exact. When the whole story unraveled. When big people got involved at the request of a government minister who, in turn, had involved himself not through the lawyers but through a friend of the Kimanis who sat in the House of Lords and was determined to get to the bones of this awful humiliation. This is how it came to light that Flannery Green had reported Thandi to a security officer at Heathrow, informing him that she was all but certain that the lady in question was hiding drugs in her pots of creams. And this is what the officer had passed on to the men who had carried out Thandi's arrest. Later, when the woman hired to investigate the whole thing paid Flannery a visit in Lichfield, Flannery would deny that she'd made false claims: "I'm a good woman, a good neighbor, you can ask around. I didn't lie, I just got it wrong."

In the end, nothing happened to Flannery. But the officers were suspended for misconduct and for failure to follow protocol. Kimani thought it didn't go far enough. He'd wanted the officers sacked. He'd been so angry, angrier than Thandi. But a few days after her return from Boston—as she lay in the sun on the veranda of their Karen home and recalled, with laughter, her mighty imprecation—she'd said to him that it was time to forget about it, that she'd taken care of them in her own way. That they would reap what they'd sown.

———————

Khaddafina Mbabazi is a writer and musician. She was a Henry Hoyns Fellow at The University of Virginia, where she received her MFA. Her work has appeared in the *Virginia Quarterly Review*, *The Johannesburg Review of Books*, and *Vox Populi*. She currently resides in Kampala, where she is working on a novel and completing a story collection.

EDITOR'S NOTE

Every now and then, a character's voice captures me right away. Stanley's story, "The List," opens with a narrator talking to his sister. Then the heart-breaking conflict unfolds. A man has lost his only child to a tragic accident and might lose his wife and marriage in the grieving aftermath.

The narrator, his sister, and his wife are fully realized characters who turn in a circle of directions after the child's death, to literature, philosophy, mysticism, and physical estrangement and retreat. Each suffers in a particular way. More than that, the characters are self-contained and revealed, known and unfolding mysteries, who grieve apart but who remain connected. When the narrator and his wife eventually reunite, a baby has already been made. The story's resolution is surprising, magical, and well earned.

Suzanne Heagy, Fiction Editor
Kestrel

THE LIST

Stanley Patrick Stocker

NOT LONG AFTER the accident, my sister Claire and I took a walk down by the river when the leaves were just beginning to turn. This was back when my wife, Eunice, was still barely getting out of bed in the mornings, and Claire had come down from Ohio to help out. As we walked, she said the soul drops down into the body anywhere from six months before birth to one month after. In the latter case, she said, it often hovers above the child, trying to decide whether to come down. I just gave her a look, and we walked on in silence, the leaves crunching beneath our feet.

To be fair, she's been into that kind of thing since we were kids. When my friends and I were in the basement smoking weed and listening to the latest Earth, Wind & Fire, she was up in her room with her girlfriends, trying to figure out what it meant if your rising sign was in Cancer. Later, after college, she became a serious meta-physician long before it was popular: crystals, a miniature pyramid in a corner of her living room big enough for her to sit beneath and "listen to the vibrations of the earth." Now she's got a decent real estate business with a Reiki practice on the side. Anyway, it sounded like so much mumbo jumbo to me. I'm a college professor, for God's sake.

That night I drove her in the rain to the bus station in a

rundown section of northeast D.C. for her trip back to Cincinnati and her husband and two pimply kids. When I got back, I went down to the dimly lit room in the basement I use as an office and tried to work on my long overdue book on Melville. I argue that *Moby-Dick* is a marvelous and variegated outward journey: Ahab shaking his fist at God and Fate and the smallness of the soul in the face of an overwhelming cosmos. "Call me Ishmael," the narrator says, but what is his real name, and what is he running from? From what crime, real or imagined? I contend that Melville veers away from a yet-untold story in allowing Ahab to take center stage so that Ishmael becomes a bystander in his own tale. What might Ishmael's journey have looked like if he were the hero? What was the source of that "damp, drizzly November" of the soul? Why was there nothing to interest him on land? Where was his mother when he was put to bed for sixteen long hours for some household infraction by a "stepmother"? I've tried to answer these questions, but for the past year I've been hopelessly stuck. Already the book was six months late and getting later by the day.

Instead of working on the manuscript, I opened my computer and paged through a couple of Melville monographs, then clicked open a folder with my name on it that Claire must have created before she left. I found a link to a website called The Philosopher's Stone, and among the topics was a discussion of how *The Odyssey* was a coded record of the journey of the soul. But there was also a discussion of how a child can come into your life for a lifetime or a few years for its own experience or for the experience of its parents. Six hours later I was deep in the rabbit hole, devouring articles about how the forty-seventh problem of Euclid, the Pythagoras Theorem, is a metaphor for the making of a child as it takes something from the mother and something from the father to create a new being. Who knew that's what we were talking about in tenth-grade geometry with Mr. Schwartz chomping on an apple and flexing his buttocks as he declaimed the beauty of $a^2 + b^2 = c^2$? You know Pythagoras supposedly died at the hands of his enemies rather than escape through a sacred bean field? The poor bastard. He's tortured thousands of high school students with his theorem, but two thousand years ago they ran him through because he'd rather die than trample a bunch of beans.

We came close to divorcing, my wife and I. Everyone thought we would, including me. What's left after something like that? Each day's a reminder of what was. She tried to deny it, but I know she blamed me. And I blamed her some, too. You picked the babysitter, I would say, over coffee that sat cold in the kitchen. You told her it was okay to take her to the playground when I said she should stay in, she would say.

After a while what's left to say? Nothing, I thought. I didn't see the point in bringing it up. What's done is done. And Eunice had long ago given up on trying to get me to talk about it in any real way. She went to stay with her sister in Baltimore, the one that's a nurse. She had an old beau there from her high school days, too, but I pretended not to remember that. I stayed at the house and, after the two months off the department gave me, I went back to work, teaching critical theory and the early modern poets at the college. My TAs treated me like the walking dead, and my colleagues, especially the ones with kids, were super solicitous, at first at least, taking me to lunch and offering to help out with my course load. Then sure as shit they asked just enough questions about the particulars to assure themselves that it couldn't happen to them. I listened and told them what they wanted to hear. Why not? I knew they could be me in a flash. Hell, they *were* me except for a handful of contingencies, none of which they had a rat's ass's control over: a left turn instead of a right, one drink more, one second less.

Sally from administration came over one afternoon just after the New Year, when it was unseasonably warm and you could imagine that spring was just around the corner. We had gone out a couple of times when I first started at the school—this was before I met Eunice—but it never really took. Well, after a few drinks and some talk about how piss-poor the office of administration was and how she really wanted to go west and help open up a medical marijuana dispensary, we went up to the bedroom and did what grown folks do. You could tell it was out of pity or something that looked like it, devouring me with those great big eyes of hers, as if she were trying to impart something that would stay with me after she left. You know: fragments to shore against my ruin. But all I could think about was that little baby hovering in the air, trying to decide whether to come down or not. Then there was Mr. Schwartz flexing his ass cheeks at the front of geometry class, and I started to laugh right then and there with Sally's lovely breasts bouncing up and down above me. The next time I saw her at the office, she told me it was her last day. She had accepted a position as the registrar at a college in Portland, her hometown.

I fell into a routine: teaching classes in the mornings and afternoons and then going down into the windowless basement to pretend to work on the book. After a while I couldn't even pretend. I printed out the manuscript and stacked it high right next to my unpublished novel. I put the Melville manuscript on a shelf close enough to my desk so I could see it, but not so close that I felt compelled to actually pick it up. Instead, I read everything I had resisted touching in the early days of educating myself. Books that could have come straight off my sister's shelf, like Jung's *Memories,*

Dreams, Reflections or Rilke's *Book of Hours: Love Poems to God*. Anything I could get my hands on having to do with myth. Sometimes I read straight through the night, or else I'd pass out at my desk. Then I got up, showered, and started all over again the next day. This went on for months.

I had no great love of critical theory, and the Melville book was an attempt to move closer to what truly interested me while remaining true at least in name to my literary focus. At heart I'm more a poetry man—modern or old, it didn't much matter—but poetry PhDs are a dime a dozen. Critical theory was simply the most logical path to tenure, though that didn't make it any easier. According to Eunice, choosing such a literary focus is like asking the girl you aren't particularly fond of to the dance because you think she's more likely to say yes, instead of the one you really want to take but are too afraid to ask. After a while you get so used to that way of thinking that you forget what it was you really wanted in the first place.

It was Eunice many years later who reminded me of the Melville idea when I was casting about for a subject for my dissertation. It was something I had shared with her at a café downtown on Eleventh Street on one of our first dates. Afterward, we went to a play and then sat on a bench at Freedom Plaza beneath the statue of that Polish military commander Kazimierz Pulaski and talked for hours, about her upbringing out in California and my growing up in Jersey. Then we walked the two miles north to her place near U Street and stood outside her building as I waited in vain for her to ask me up.

We had met at a "fix-up" dinner in which friends invited other friends who they thought might be a good match for someone else in the group. I was paired with a young math professor who sat to my left while Eunice, an economist at the World Bank, sat to my right. It wasn't until after dinner when we all went bowling that I really noticed Eunice. I was standing in those ridiculous shoes they make you wear, about to take my turn, when I felt a heat at my lower back. Right then and there I thought, "Whoever is behind me digs me," so I turned and there was Eunice about twenty feet away, talking to one of the other women. She turned and looked at me for a moment. Afterward, I went up to her, and we started talking. That night a friend gave us a ride home, and we exchanged numbers after learning that we worked two blocks from each other.

It was maybe two months into our courtship that I thought maybe it wouldn't work out. More and more it began to bother me that she would never let me pay for her during our dates. Whether it was dinner or a movie, she was always quick to pull out her wallet. We were at a little French restaurant for lunch in Georgetown when once again she reached for her wallet, insisting on paying for herself. By then I knew it was her way of not letting me get too close, and I sat in silence as I ate and denied that anything was wrong when she asked. As we walked past the Dumbarton Oaks gardens, I told her I was upset because she never let me pay for her. We went back and forth for a while, but finally she said she never let me pay because she was afraid of getting hurt and burst out in tears. "I don't know if love is real," she said. "Whether it can last." I told her it could, that I knew it could, but we'd have to open ourselves up to it. That night we went to bed together for the first time and got engaged at that park two years later.

Eventually, Eunice came back from Baltimore and her sister's. I came home one day after grading papers at the neighborhood coffee shop, and her hatchback was sitting in the drive with the BABY ON BOARD sign that I always hated. Or used to, at least. She'd found the sign at a garage sale when she was six months pregnant. "Why are babies any more precious than grown-ups?" I said, as she paid the man with wadded-up bills from her wallet. Why not Human Being On Board? Or Used to Be a Baby On Board? Eunice said I was overthinking it, and babies are babies, and we should take care of them. Still I argued the point, but I sang a different tune after my own baby came along, that was for sure.

A few days after she was born she needed a procedure. Nothing serious, just something to do with her skin that they might as well take care of while they had her, but when they didn't bring her back at the expected time? Man, I just knew something had gone bad. Worse, I knew something had gone bad and they were already in cover-up mode. "Where is she? Why isn't she back yet?" I said, surprising everyone, including myself, by bursting into tears. The nurses just stared at me like they were embarrassed and said they didn't know. That's when this other nurse wheeled her in in her little metal bassinet, and she was fine. Apparently, it was a big weekend for giving birth, coming nine months after that Snowmageddon storm that had shut down the city for weeks, and they just couldn't get her in the OR because of the assload of babies being born that weekend.

The day Eunice got back from Baltimore, I went inside to find her sitting in the living room, sipping a cup of coffee and watching the news. Well, not watching exactly, more like the news was on, and she was staring in the direction of the TV. Her things were still standing in the entryway, so I took them upstairs and un-packed them. I hadn't changed anything so it was no trouble. And I didn't tell her about Sally, either, and also I didn't ask about her six months in Baltimore. What's good for the goose, as my old man used to say. For a couple of weeks, there were calls on Eunice's cell that she always took in the other room, or she would cut them short after a few seconds. I didn't feel it was my place to ask, no matter how curious I was about them. After a while the calls died down, and we pretty much picked up where we'd left off.

Before, it had been hard to find time to make love, or space even. Who knew a kid could take up so much room in a bed? At the end of the day, Eunice and I always fell into bed exhausted, and the kid seemed to sleep better with us, so we didn't fight it. Pretty soon she refused to sleep anywhere else. After the accident we had all the time and space in the world and none of the inclination.

Often before Eunice left for Baltimore, she would stop down in the basement and ask if I wanted anything to eat. Most times I didn't, but I'd go up anyway. That's the way it was between us: she'd ask if I was hungry, and I lied and said yes. It was the only thing we had to say to each other, so we'd sit there and push our food around our plates until it looked like we'd eaten, if you weren't paying particular attention. Then after a while we'd clear the dishes, and I'd wash them.

Don't get me wrong; I put on nearly forty pounds in the months after the accident, I ate so much, but it was always on the run, between classes, or I'd grab something—a pizza, sometimes two, or a sub—while grading papers, but not at home, never at home. Sometimes I didn't even remember eating or feeling hungry. I just ate like it was a job. Of course, none of my clothes fit, and I'd walk around campus looking like a tramp in these expandable-waist slacks and full-cut shirts I picked up at the Big and Tall.

Eunice was just the opposite. She ate so little she'd dwindled down to some distilled essence, as if everything superficial had been burned away and what remained was fierce and raw and naked as an unsheathed sword. Sometimes I'd wonder if maybe she felt that if our kid couldn't be here to eat, then she wouldn't eat either, though it hardly seemed to require much effort on her part, this denial. When I'd ask, she'd just say most times she'd just forgotten to eat. Once I went into the kitchen and found her standing in front of the refrigerator with the door open. I went upstairs to get something I had forgotten and came back down, and she was still standing there. When I asked what she was doing, she said, "Betraying her, that's what." It freaked me out so much that I lied and said I had class, though it didn't start for another two hours. I ended up driving around for over an hour before I steered the car toward campus.

It was Eunice who had pushed to have a kid. I was game in theory. But doing and thinking are two different things, and after a year of trying without any luck, we decided to get some help of the professional kind. My boys were a little on the old side, but in good enough shape generally, though the doctor said a certain percentage had what he called "abnormalities." Apparently, some of them were just swimming around in circles like little idiots, which was a little disconcerting. Eunice and I had a good laugh about that.

"See, that's why we're not pregnant yet," she'd say. "Your fellas are running around in circles like drunkards!" Then she'd stagger around the kitchen like she had one too many. Or she'd limp around with an umbrella in her hand like Charlie Chaplin and say, "Who am I? Who am I? Your sperm, that's who!" She always did have a sense of humor.

Eunice herself was solid, being almost fifteen years younger—not that that's a guarantee of anything. But man, nobody talks about how hard it'll be even with the pros involved: the needles, the bruising, the tears, running out in the middle of the night because you've got the wrong size needle and you have to give a particular shot at a particular time or you're screwed. For a long time we wondered, Why us? But in the end I thought, Hell, why not us? Why should this pass by our door and land at someone else's? Melville and his universal thump, that's what.

We went through a boatload of money, consulting different doctors. The first time we saw this one guy he spoke to Eunice the whole time without even looking my way, like I was the Invisible Fucking Man when I was sitting right there next to her. I picked up my coat, and we were out. Second place we tried and got pregnant, but it lasted maybe six days? Seriously. I used to use my notebook to keep track of where we were in the process.

It was around then that I started writing down key pieces from literature or music or film that somehow made me feel better, even if just to confirm how truly shitty things could get. A list of greatest hits, if you will. Whitman's "Crossing Brooklyn Ferry" always makes me wonder whether my long-dead mother might just be looking at me now, for all I cannot see her. Lincoln's Gettysburg Address, because you have to have some beauty around you at all times. Anne Sexton and her *Awful Rowing Toward God* with the oarlocks sticking and the sea blinking and rolling "like a worried eyeball." That scene in Fellini's 8½ where Mastroianni's dreaming of his boyhood days bathing with all the other little boys in those enormous tubs. Ellington's "Concerto for Cootie," because if you ever want to forget your troubles and imagine yourself dressed to the nines walking down the street without a care in the world, then that's the piece for you. Heck, if Adam and Eve had a theme song for that time in the Garden before all that unpleasantness began, then that would have to be it.

Those were just a few of the things that made up the list.

Somehow having it near me at all times made me feel better. Untouchable even.

Around that time, the doctors at that practice started jumping ship like the place was on fire. One after the other. Meanwhile, they were hosing out our bank account. There were always enough of them left to make sure that got done. After a while we asked the doctor, the head of the practice, whether it was time to call it a day and try adoption. "But that's not what you want," he said. "Let's give it another try." And I think he genuinely wanted to help. We had come so close so many times. There were even twins once. That lasted about a week. We went down to the church and lit candles for them. Even named them. But one more shot? We looked at each other and said, Sure, let's give it another try. "Run it on back again," Eunice said.

Then finally everything went well. Too well. There were too many eggs, and they were too big. Eunice had overstimulated, and if he gave her the final trigger shot, it could mean serious health problems. We pulled the plug on that "last final round," at that particular clinic at least. And you know what the doctor asked at one of the final meetings?

"Do you keep records of all your doctor consults in that book?" And he pointed down at my notebook like it was a criminal summons with his name on it. "Is that what that is?" he asked.

"No, I'm an English teacher, and most of these are my notes for class."

Then I thought about all of those rats jumping ship while we were there; maybe they were afraid of getting sued.

I always thought if I had a kid, it would be a boy. I just took it for granted. Then she came along. The IVF finally took. The weird thing is it was Dr. Invisible Man who made it happen after we went back to him. And she was a daddy's girl almost right off the bat. If she took a tumble or was afraid or angry, it was me she'd come running to. Me she'd cuddle up next to and near push out of the bed at night, arms all akimbo. It hurt my wife's feelings that she wasn't the main one, as if she were lacking something as a mom. But that wasn't it. Maybe it had something to do with the fact that my mother died when I was a kid, but once she came, boy, I took to her like she was the sun and the moon.

On those long winter nights when Eunice was away, I'd sometimes call my sister to talk about the things I read and thought about when I was down there in the basement. How the pyramids, stretching as they do from four-cornered earth to sky, are symbolic of humankind's destined unity with God; how some scholars talked about reincarnation and how it just might be right there in the Bible if you knew where to look. She'd listen patiently. It's a tenet of her faith, and one she honors, not to judge someone who isn't as far along on the path as she is. A tree towering in the forest never looks down on the little sapling in the clearing. I'm grateful for that. So when I told her there seems to be story after story of the soul plunging down in a kind of mad, willful ignorance and slowly making its way up to the light, I could actually feel her smiling on the other end of the line, as if warmth could be sent like light across a wire.

"I understand," she'd say. "Yes, I understand."

And sometimes I'd tell her my dreams, something I hadn't done since we were kids together in that little house down on Sylvania Avenue that our folks bought two or three years before our mother died, and our world exploded, after which Claire seemed to head down one path in life and I down another.

In one dream, I'm driving and the kid's in the car seat behind me, facing backward. (My wife and I had a knock-down-drag-out about how long the car seat needed to be facing backward, by the way. As long as possible, it turns out, given their pencil-thin necks and the driving skills of the average resident of our fair city.) Anyway, the kid and I are taking turns listening to my music and then hers, mine then hers, switching back and forth. That's it. I'm just listening as she laughs and asks me what instrument it is when my music is playing. Or me singing some song or other or telling her that in a little bit on my side of the car there'll be a yellow school bus or one of those construction vehicles she loves so much. In the dream, it's sunny and warm, and we're traveling along the parkway with the windows down.

I had the exact same dream a couple of weeks after Eunice returned, but this time she was in the car too. We were driving down the same stretch of the parkway, the three of us laughing and talking.

When I woke up, I turned to my daughter in the bed between us, it felt so real. Then I ran to the window to look out at the car, even though I knew I had put the car seat away in the garage along with that other stuff boxed up there gathering dust.

I knew at that moment that if I didn't tell Eunice everything about the dream, I would die. Not actually die, of course, but in that slow inexorable way that men die daily, the kind of death that leaves families broken and marriages empty. So I told her the dream as we lay there in bed: what our daughter was wearing; how her voice sounded; how warm it was outside. Eunice asked for an ever-increasing level of detail: Did she seem happy? (Yes.) Had she eaten? (She had a bag of sour cream chips, I think.) Did she have on her cream-colored jacket? (No, a jumper, blue with some kind of animal on the bib. I can't be sure.) Some of the details I supplied without knowing whether they were real or whether I was making them up as I went along.

Then for a long, long time we just lay there with a breeze coming through the window. It was late spring by then; the warm weather had arrived for real. Then, I can't say why but I reached out and touched her arm with the tips of my fingers and, I don't know, just waited. A lot of people think once you're married it no longer takes any kind of courage to express your desire, but sometimes it can be just as scary as the first time: I didn't have the slightest idea how she'd react. Or exactly what it was that I wanted. But eventually she put her hand on mine, and our hands slowly intertwined, moving together and letting go and intertwining again, as if we were circling some invisible thing between us.

It was like that first time we went to the movies together on our first date, sitting there in the darkness. Not long after, she told me she had thought it was corny at first, the way I caressed her hand, but then she said everything else fell away and it was only our hands, moving together in the darkness. It was like that again now, except it was her body and mine, slowly moving, intertwining and reconfiguring in the half-light of early morning.

Like a knife, she cut through the layers of fatted flesh down to where my wounded heart had hidden itself and, once exposed, oh, I wailed for my lost little one, and Eunice, she burrowed into that flaccid flesh, and I covered her naked grief as best I could as she wept, and we spoke her name over and over again: *Veaunita, Veaunita, Veaunita*. Then sleep—long and hard and dreamless— descended upon us and relieved us of our names.

When we woke in the late afternoon, I was the one who asked if she was hungry. She said she was, and I knew she meant it. And I was too and keenly aware of it. I'm no cook, but growing up in Jersey my dad was famous for the breakfast he'd make. It was one of the things he passed on to me. So I fired up the stove and made hickory-smoked bacon, scrapple, eggs sunny-side up, grits, pancakes, Belgian waffles, real whole-wheat biscuits from scratch, fruit salad, and a side salad with dressing. Hot coffee and fresh-squeezed orange juice. As I cooked something, I put whatever I had finished in the oven to keep warm. Then, after everything was done and the table was groaning under the weight of it all, we eyed each other across the table and dug in as if it were for the first time ever, or maybe the last, sopping up the bright yellow yolk of the eggs with the biscuits until they were dripping, washing it down with hot coffee, wolfing down the fruit with our hands, stuffing slabs of pancakes in our mouths.

Our hunger was inexhaustible, bottomless, with neither beginning nor end.

When every plate was empty and piled one on top of the other, we sat there in silence, happy for once. Then after a while Eunice looked over at me and said, "Run it back again, Charlie Chaplin. Run it back." I looked at her to see if she was serious and she gave me a look, and I knew she meant it, so I turned on the stove again.

Seven months later, we were back in the same hospital as before, and Eunice gave birth to a healthy baby girl. Yeah, I know what you're thinking. I can do the math. But it doesn't matter. Like my old man says, what's good for the goose is good for the gander.

When the baby was three months old we took her to Baltimore to meet Eunice's sister. Steven, the old beau, was there, too. He stood with his hands in his pockets, waiting, it seemed, for someone to tell him it was all right for him to be there, even though Eunice had expressly said she wanted him there. When she lay the baby in his arms, he cradled her like a little doll.

"She's light as air," he said smiling, then repeated it. "She's light as air." Then he passed her back to Eunice, still smiling, and shoved his hands in his pockets and hopped lightly from foot to foot, saying, "She's as light as a feather."

One day we'll explain it all to her—how, long ago, an old man would rather die than cross a sacred bean field, and how a baby decided to come to us, to her old man and her mama, in this time and this place and in this manner, to spend a little while or all of our lifetimes by our side. In the meantime, I hold her in my arms and devour her with my eyes.

———

Stanley Patrick Stocker's fiction has appeared in *Kestrel* and *Middle House Review*. He received an Individual Artist Award in Fiction from the Maryland State Arts Council. Originally from Philadelphia, Stanley lives with his wife and son in the Washington, D.C., area, where he practices law. A graduate of Amherst College and Harvard Law School, he is currently working on a novel. He can be found at stanleypatrickstocker.com.

EDITOR'S NOTE

Zhang's story, "Mandy's Mary Sue," was submitted as part of *sinθ* magazine's summer writing contest. We had three prompts: "Set your written piece inside a cube"; "speculative futures"; and the following quote from the character Dr. Yu Tsun in Jorge Luis Borges's "The Garden of Forking Paths": "I thought of a labyrinth of labyrinths, of one sinuous spreading labyrinth that would encompass the past and the future and in some way involve the stars." I like to think that Zhang fulfilled all three prompts with this funny, relatable, and engaging story about a young girl's coming of age. Not only does Mandy literally invent futures for herself, but her relationship to her identity is mediated through the magical cube that is her computer, which provides access to labyrinths within labyrinths of information, abundant and contradictory, sending Mandy spiraling into confusion yet providing solid anchors, using which she is able to begin deciding what kind of person she wants to be.

Reading "Mandy's Mary Sue," I was immediately struck by the strength of Zhang's voice, the sustained, cyclical narrative, and the deft, almost effortless manner in which Zhang is able to sketch out this cast of characters. The story certainly reminded me of my own misadventures with anime and DeviantArt at Mandy's age, and I'm sure that it will resonate with any reader who has spent any amount of time in an internet black hole, wondering what all these pixels amount to. "Mandy's Mary Sue" was short-listed for *sinθ*'s fiction prize, and judge K-Ming Chang said: "It's full of language we can't look away from: bodily, visceral, meaty, refusing to shy away . . . It comments so powerfully on desire, dis/embodiment, imagination and fantasy."

Jiaqi Kang, Editor in Chief
sinθ magazine

MANDY'S MARY SUE

Qianze Zhang

MANDY DONG WAS only nine years old when she got her first period. By that time, she was also two years ahead of her class in math and had already been watching pornography for three months. Mandy watched porn on her family's only desktop monitor, in a room that most white families would call a "study" but her family called "the computer room." She preferred videos that showed women without men, because the sight of an erect penis horrified and confused her. When she browsed the thumbnails, she averted her eyes from the smooth rods of flesh disappearing halfway into another body. As she watched the beautiful women, she would passionately kiss the back of her hand, focusing first on the pressure felt on her lips, then on the softness felt on her hand, trying to understand what it was like to both give and receive. Each time she finished, she closed the browser tab, then erased the history, cookies, and cache from the past day. When she wasn't careful and the porn websites installed malware on her family's computer, she knew how to move the appropriate files to the trash and empty the bin, the resulting sound effect of rustling paper calming her small, hot core of anxiety.

At first, when Mandy noticed the mysterious red spots appearing on the crotch of her underwear, she was able to ignore them.

Subconsciously, she understood that some people would see this as reckless. But Mandy was able to brush it off because she thought herself exceptional. Not in the way musical prodigies and toddlers excelling at acrobatics lessons are exceptional, but also not tragically exceptional, like unlucky children who have extremely rare diseases and die from them. Mandy knew she lay tepidly somewhere in the middle—she was exceptional because she managed to get straight As even with her porn and cartoon habits, because all her friends were boys, and because she was alarmingly good at drawing adult bodies even though hers was far from one. So the blood couldn't have been anything serious.

It took her mother doing laundry on Sunday morning and discovering the multiple pairs of dappled underwear for her to finally address it. Mandy remained unconcerned, even when her mother called her name, her voice vibrating with a shrillness usually reserved for her father when he came home too late in the evening from work, pork fat condensed into beads on his brow. When the shrillness first appeared, about four years after their wedding day, he resented it because he didn't want to accept that his wife was turning into his mother-in-law, who also used to be beautiful, and whose voice rang like a rooster's cry every morning to jolt open the eyes of her neighbors and feed the sun to their irises.

Mandy's mother ushered her into the bedroom. They sat down on the edge of the creaky mattress, the weight of her mother's body forming a crater that Mandy nearly slid into. "*Mantee*—" she hesitated, and Mandy finally felt a spike of anxiety, worrying that a porn virus manifested without her knowing or that she forgot to clear her browsing history. "You are getting your period, which is a normal part of growing up."

"I know," responded Mandy. Which was strange, because she

didn't know. She meant that she knew that it was normal, and that everything was fine, and that she had heard of puberty before— the older girls at Chinese church once lifted their shirts up and invited her to feel their bras, the cool, slippery satin punctuated by cheap lace trimming. She knew what a bra was, and she knew that a brazilla was a bra that was just really big. She knew that her private parts weren't broken, and anything she didn't know, she could probably figure out by googling, so there was really no need for this conversation with her mother.

Despite Mandy already knowing, her mother continued with a demonstration. There was a menstrual pad and a pair of panties in her mother's lap. She removed the pad's pale yellow wrapper and peeled off the small, individual pieces of plastic covering the wings, then wrapped them around the crotch of the panties. Mandy was familiar with these little foam squares. When she had to dig around for a new toothbrush or bar of soap in the bathroom sink cabinet, she often saw an opened bag of them with a few spilling out like oversized confetti. Once, next to the pads, she saw a large jar of supplements. By googling the brand name on the label, she learned that they were breast augmentation supplements. Mandy hated knowing this about her mother. It wasn't because she was uncomfortable thinking about her mother's breasts. She'd seen them by accident before and thought they looked regular. She wondered if her own nipples would also one day enlarge into Rolo candies. The discovery of the supplements disappointed Mandy because her beautiful mother, who never commented on Mandy's appearance, who never wore makeup, not even on her wedding day, who scoffed at TV infomercials and taught her to do the same, was taking bogus herbal supplements to augment her breasts.

Later that night, Mandy was in the computer room again, this time on a website for watching serialized cartoons. Mandy preferred cartoons where men were the main characters and female characters merely flanked them. She liked having room to invent her own female character who stood out against the other women who were too weak, too ugly, or too bogged down by their feelings for a man. She took great pride and care in this process, taking time between watching episodes to contemplate how this new character could fit into the existing plot, forming a faint mental image of her expression, the line work of her limbs, crystalizing this new member of a universe by drawing a portrait of her in the style of the original cartoonist.

For the past week, Mandy had been working on a female character for a cartoon where humans have magical powers and use them to battle one another. The existing female characters underwhelmed Mandy because their powers felt passive, mostly used for healing and supporting other characters on the front lines of battle. So Mandy drew a woman whose long legs and skimpy black costume screamed "I'll cut you!" Her hair was styled in a ponytail with two long strands on either side of her face, hanging on like garter snakes. She was armed with short knives for close-range combat and her power was mind control, but she didn't always need to use it because her sexual charm was often powerful enough against her male opponents.

Mandy still had to choose a name for her new character. She googled "japanese baby names." The first result took her to a flat, pink-and-blue website with hundreds of names organized in alphabetical order. She started down the list. *Ai*: Mandy knew this name meant *love*. It was too short, and promised too much. *Aiko, Aimi, Aina, Airi*. These names were too cutesy and pink. Her character was a badass. She figured any *A* name would be

too predictable. She skipped forward to the *M* names: *Mitsuko,*
Miyoko, Momoko—Mandy knew she had found the one. Three
syllables was the Goldilocks length, and Momoko could even be
shortened to Momo, a perfectly darling nickname to be used by
characters who were lucky enough to be close to her.

Mandy felt like an intruder browsing the Japanese names when
she wasn't even Japanese. When her classmates asked her "What's
my Chinese name?" she would respond, "You don't have one, your
parents have to give you one right when you're born. You missed
your chance." But Chinese names were usually just three syllables
total, lacking grace, easily bastardized. She especially disliked her
surname, so easily appropriated for the salacious entertainment of
the grade school boys she spent most of her days with: Dong! It
dully bounced off the tongue, like an irreverent sound effect in a
slapstick comedy. The best cases were Zhang or Xiao, names that
took what Americans thought was their alphabet and twisted it
in unexpected ways, eluding mockery through cunning. Japanese
names, on the other hand, had six, eight, even ten syllables, and
seemed untouchable because the average American attention span
is unable to make it past the first three.

Momoko was everything Mandy wished she could be. She had
flaws programmed into her for narrative plausibility, but Mandy
still saw her as perfect. Porn did not exist in Momoko's universe,
but if it did, she would not watch it. Momoko, did, however, have
sex, but just the right amount, which meant selectively, just with
one man, who happened to be the character Mandy had a crush on.
She also had a period, Mandy guessed, but it didn't need a place in
the plot. Mandy lulled herself to sleep by inventing scenarios from
Momoko's universe in her head, scenarios that perfectly showcased
just how desirable-but-didn't-know-it she was. She was the best of

every binary, even when that meant embodying two opposites. She sometimes needed to be saved by men but also occasionally saved them back; she was an outcast but loved by many; her skin was scratched from combat but terribly smooth, cel shaded, only two colors, highlight and shadow.

The next morning, Mandy sprinted to the school bus stop. She was running late, having stayed up drawing Momoko. There was no way she was going to tell her friends about the menstruating, especially since they were all boys, a fact she took pride in but was just beginning to see the disadvantages of. For one, she would frequently develop crushes on them. The crushes waxed and waned and pinballed from boy to boy, but since the beginning of the school year in September, Mandy had her eyes on Chase, a shy boy with droopy eyes. It was now March, petals were dropping from the trees and being stomped into damp mush on the sidewalks, and Mandy hadn't so much as dropped a hint.

In the schoolyard, where all the students collected in the morning before being funneled to their classrooms, Mandy retrieved her markers and the drawing of Momoko from her backpack to add a few details to her outfit. A small crowd formed around her to watch.

One girl inquired, "Is that you?" and Mandy didn't know how to answer.

A nasally voice blurted, "She looks like a lesbian," and Mandy huffed defensively, "She's not even!"

Then, Mandy heard Chase's voice from behind her, "She's pretty. Can I have her?"

She answered coolly, "Okay, when I'm done with it." *Her name is Momoko, but you can call me Momo.*

Some time that afternoon, during the purgatory between recess and the bell ending the school day, Mandy asked for the bathroom pass and left the classroom with a pad tucked into the pocket of her hoodie. First she went inside the middle stall and peed. She took the pad out of its pastel yellow wrapping and peeled off the small sheets of plastic covering the wings, then wrapped them around the crotch of her panties. She washed her hands, then studied her face in the mirror. She gathered her coarse black hair into a ponytail, then nudged out two strands at the front, one framing each side of her face, hanging like garter snakes.

Qianze Zhang is a multidisciplinary artist working across painting, writing, and digital media. She studied computer science and fine arts at the University of Southern California. She is a child of Chinese immigrants and lives in Washington State. Currently, she's interested in how the information age uniquely mutates memory and complicates coming-of-age narratives.

EDITOR'S NOTE

An earlier version of "Taxi" made it to the final round of consideration for publication. I was impressed with the economy of the writing and the honesty of the narrative voice. The characters were convincing and fresh. These were characters on the margin, struggling to survive, characters that do not often appear in the stories we receive: an unlicensed taxi driver putting himself through school, a woman and her young son trying to get to a fast-food restaurant. The characters and the situation intrigued me, but in the final analysis the story was not quite where it needed to be or as good as it could be.

A year later, I was pleased to see the story reappear among the submissions. I was even more pleased with the revision. The author had revised the story, addressing my concerns with the ending. This revised version was accepted for publication and it was one of our nominations for the Pushcart Prize. The boy's jacket, which in the first draft had seemed inconsequential, emerged as an element central to this quietly haunting story. The story reveals the dignity and humanity of people struggling to survive, and like all great stories it retains a sense of mystery that extends beyond these few pages.

I am always thrilled to publish a writer for the first time, particularly those writers who continue to write and publish well. Pardeep Toor is one of those writers from whom I expect we will hear more in the future. I look forward to reading more of his work.

Christopher Chambers, Editor
Midwest Review

TAXI

Pardeep Toor

HANS PARKED THE yellow cab in front of a lime green house near the central part of the city, amid the cheaply constructed square municipal buildings. He fumbled with the lever to adjust the seat. He pushed forward, backward, and then forward again until he felt comfortable with the space between his knees and the steering wheel. He put both his hands on the steering wheel and pretended to drive.

Hans didn't own the cab. He had borrowed it from his friend Kanti. Hans and Kanti had gone to high school together. Kanti's dad gave him the yellow cab after he dropped out of high school. Hans drove the cab during weekday mornings and afternoons. Kanti preferred nights and weekends when business was best. Kanti left the car in the school parking lot every morning before teachers, secretaries, or anyone who could recognize him arrived. He left the keys under the driver's seat mat. Hans attended algebra class at nine in the morning, but then skipped English at ten. He didn't read well enough to understand or discuss the stories in class so he preferred to drive the taxi for an hour every morning. Hans returned to school in the afternoon for gym class.

Hans looked at the house. There were two large windows on either side of the door. A red light shined through the holes in the brown curtain on one of the windows. Cracks in the other window resembled a spider's web. The front door opened. The windows shook when it slammed shut. A woman stepped out of the house clutching a young boy by the hood of his navy blue bubble jacket. She pulled the hood for balance. The boy's head jerked back in her grasp with each step but his eyes remained focused on the icy asphalt in front of them. She hesitated down the stairs, especially the bottom wooden plank that was propped up with crumbling bricks. The path from their front door to the cab was muddled with slush and small piles of dirty snow.

The woman fell into the cab as she reached for the door. She pulled the handle. The door didn't open. Hans's shoulder cracked when he reached for the lock. The woman slapped the rear window. Hans lifted the lock up. The woman pulled the door open and stepped back a few steps. The boy ducked and spun in a circle to free himself from the woman.

"Get over here," the woman said. The boy's tiny hand grazed the hood of the cab as he ran to the passenger-side door. He wasn't tall enough to reach the window, so he knocked on the door.

"Open up, mister," the boy said.

Hans unlocked the door. The boy jumped into the car.

"Get in the back with me," the woman said.

The woman struggled to place herself in the back seat. She dove into the car headfirst. Her baseball cap fell as she first sprawled across the seat on her stomach before dragging her feet in. She pushed herself up off the seat. She adjusted her bleached jeans at the knees before sitting upright. She put her hat back on. Her stringy hair protruded from the rim of the hat and matted her bangs over her forehead.

"I'm fine up here, Mom. Mister doesn't mind," the boy said.

"I don't mind," Hans said.

The woman reached over the front passenger seat to buckle her son's seat belt. Her eyes were red, and an odorous cloud engulfed Hans with familiarity and disgust. The odor, her unsteady hand, anxious fingers, and scars on her cheeks evoked nostalgia in Hans.

"Where can I take you on this wonderful Tuesday morning?" Hans said, in accordance with the script Kanti provided him. He made eye contact with the woman through the rearview mirror.

"Where do you want to go?" the woman said, poking the boy in the arm.

"Burger World," he said.

"Not Burger World," she said. "Let's go to Joe's Tacos."

"But I want Burger World."

"But Mom wants tacos so we're going to Joe's," the woman said.

Hans glanced at the boy and then the woman.

"So?" Hans said.

"You do what I say and I say Joe's," the woman said.

Hans looked at the boy one more time.

"Why are you looking at him? I'm the one paying you."

"I'm sorry, ma'am," Hans said.

Hans started the meter and shifted the car into drive. The boy pulled out a plastic handheld game from his jacket pocket, a maze with a small silver marble inside. He gently maneuvered his hands to guide the marble to the hole in the center.

Hans stopped at a red light.

"Can I smoke in the car?" the woman said.

"No problem," Hans said.

Hans had smoked his last cigarette the previous summer on a riverbank, about twenty miles west of the city. Kanti took him there for a vacation day. They smoked together with their feet in the cold river water. Even in the summer the river was cold. Hans remembered the taste in his mouth from the last cigarette. He had accidentally put the lit side in his mouth. The butt left a permanent burn mark on the inside of his lips. It was the last time he had smoked or visited the river.

Hans turned to the boy, who didn't look up from his pocket game.

"Do you have a light?" the woman said.

Hans pretended to check his pockets. He opened the glove compartment in front of the boy's feet and tried to quickly close it before the empty candy wrappers fell out. A book fell at the boy's feet. The boy picked it up. On the cover was an illustration of a man and a woman, their bodies entangled. The title of the book was *Pleasurable Positions*. Hans grabbed the book and put it under his thigh. Hans looked back at the woman. She kicked Hans's seat while shuffling her legs side to side. Hans searched the compartment underneath the radio but couldn't find a lighter.

"I don't have one," Hans said. "I don't smoke anymore."

"Why did you stop smoking?" the boy said.

"Health reasons," Hans said.

"There's nothing wrong with my health," the woman said.

The boy put the handheld game in his pocket and wiped his nose with his jacket sleeve. His shirt was too small for him. His wrists were exposed to the cold. His pants were stained with mud at the knees and around the ankles. Hans turned the heat up.

"Pull over here at Mario's store. I need a lighter," the woman said.

"Where?"

"Mario's. Right here. You're passing it. Turn," the woman said.

The car slid on the ice as Hans stopped in the middle turning lane. He looked in both directions but didn't see Mario's. Cars honked at him from both directions.

"Mario's is on the next block, Mom," the boy said. "Keep going, mister."

The woman leaned forward in her seat. She placed a cigarette in her mouth and twirled another one in her fingers. "Don't you dare talk to me like that again," she said.

"I didn't say anything," the boy said.

"Like that. Just like that. Don't do it."

Hans inhaled the anticipated stench from the burning cigarette. He swallowed his built-up saliva and began to whistle in the car to mimic the act of blowing smoke through his lips. He merged with traffic and drove slowly to the next block.

"Did you use the patch, mister?" the boy said.

"What?" Hans said.

"The cigarette patch. To quit smoking."

"No, I quit on my own," Hans said. "My sister helped me. She rubbed my legs with oils all night when I was in withdrawal."

"Why doesn't your sister help us, Mom?" the boy said.

"We don't need anyone's help," she said.

"They might have a lighter over there," Hans said. He pointed to a store at the corner of the next intersection. The building's

white side panels were stained with streaks of rust from the leaking gutters. A small handwritten sign in the window said DOLLAR
PALACE.

"That's Mario's," the woman said.

"It says Dollar Palace," Hans said.

"It's Mario's," the boy said.

The woman opened the car door before Hans finished parking
and stepped into a puddle. She knocked on Hans's window. He
rolled it down.

"Do you want something? A bag of chips?" she said.

"No, thank you," Hans said. Kanti had instructed him to never
accept anything from customers.

"Can I get a bag of chips?" the boy said.

"Do you have any money?"

"No," the boy said.

"Then the answer is no."

"The meter is running," Hans called after the woman as she
walked away from the car.

Hans looked at the boy. The boy stared back.

"What's in that book?" the boy said.

"What book?"

"The one under your leg."

"It's not mine. It's my partner Kanti's."

"What's in it?"

"I don't know," Hans said.

"Is it sex?"

Hans shrugged.

"My brother told me about that stuff," the boy said.

"I haven't read it," Hans said.

"You're lying."

"How do you know?" Hans said.

"My mom is a liar. I know liars."

Hans reached into his pocket and pulled out a dollar bill. "Here, go get yourself a bag of chips."

The boy took the dollar and opened the door. He threw his jacket on the seat and sprinted into Mario's. Hans felt sorry for the boy. He was a child. He was hungry. Hans hit the buttons on the meter to try to stop the red analog numbers from ticking up but the meter couldn't be paused. Hans turned on the radio, scanned the stations, and then turned it off. Feeling claustrophobic, he rolled down his window, stuck his head out, and took a deep breath. The wind stung his gums and cheeks. The cab smelled like cigarette smoke. He searched for an air freshener under the seat but couldn't find one. He scanned the cover of the book and then put it back in the glove compartment. Hans rested his head on his window and tapped his feet to the music that was no longer playing. The salt and slush under his shoes swished from one side of the mat to the other. The door to Mario's opened and closed several times but the woman and boy were nowhere to be seen. He saw more people exit Mario's than he'd seen enter.

Hans lifted the boy's jacket off the seat. It reeked of smoke. He put it down. He picked it up again. He closed his eyes and looked away from the jacket as he squeezed it in his hand. The fabric made a squishing noise in his fist. He looked at the door to Mario's again. He lowered himself in his seat and pulled the jacket to his face. Hans inhaled the burnt smoky smell. He swirled his tongue on the inner fleece lining of the jacket. The putrid smell and taste of the fabric invigorated him, like a cup of coffee in the morning.

Hans's chest shook. He sat up and saw the door to Mario's open. The woman and the boy were yelling at each other. Each carried a small bag of chips. Hans stuffed the jacket in the glove compartment on top of the sex book.

The woman and the boy got back into the car. "Off to Burger World now," the woman said.

Hans waited for their doors to close. "I thought we were going to Joe's Tacos," Hans said.

"I want Burger World," the woman said. She held a cigarette in her lips and rolled down her window.

"You said Joe's before," the boy said.

"What did I tell you about talking back to me?"

"You said Joe's."

"I said Burger World," the woman said.

"Burger World then?" Hans said.

"I guess," the boy said.

The woman shifted forward to the edge of the seat until she was face-to-face with the boy. She grabbed the front of the boy's shirt. "I warned you about this," she said. "I warned you about talking so much." She let go of his shirt and slapped his chest softly three times.

"Turn this car around right now," she said to Hans. "We're going home."

"Mom, I didn't say anything," the boy said.

Hans looked down to see a cigarette in the cup holder between the two front seats. It must have fallen out of her mouth.

"We're going home," she said.

"Mom, please."

"Home."

Hans put the car in drive and headed toward the green house. The boy put his head in his hands.

"Don't cry," the woman said.

"I'm not crying."

"I didn't teach you to cry."

"You always do this."

"Do what?" the woman said. "What am I doing?"

"Nothing," the boy said.

"That's what I thought."

They drove the rest of the way in silence. Hans sped up at yellow lights and rolled through stop signs. He parked in front of the house and stopped the meter. "I didn't tell you to stop that meter," the woman said.

"We're home," Hans said.

"You wait here. Keep that meter going."

The woman and the boy exited the car and silently walked into the house. Hans gently picked up the cigarette from the cup holder. He was careful not to squeeze it between his thumb and index finger. The integrity of the shape was important. He examined it carefully from all angles. He sniffed it from one side to the other. He placed it in the glove compartment, beside the boy's jacket. He licked his thumb and index finger. The taste of tobacco made him salivate. The woman and boy stepped out of the house. They both got in the back seat this time.

Hans looked at himself in the rearview mirror. His cheeks were red. Flakes of dry skin smothered his chin. He looked at the boy.

"We decided on Waffle Place," the woman said.

"I'm getting the Mega Meal," the boy said.

Hans began driving toward Waffle Place. It was on the other side of town, in the opposite direction of Joe's Tacos and Burger World. He was going to be late for gym class.

Hans looked in the rearview mirror. The woman and the boy were cuddled up together. The boy smiled each time the woman tickled his arm. Hans turned on the radio. The boy stood in his seat and started dancing to the song.

"Put your seat belt on," the woman said. She pulled the boy closer and sat him down in the seat. She buckled the middle seat belt around his waist and put her arms around his shoulders. Her fingers tapped his elbow to the rhythm of the song.

Hans stopped at a red light, two blocks short of Waffle Place.

"Are you okay with the temperature?" Hans said.

"I'm cold," the boy said.

Hans directed the vents toward them and turned up the heat.

"It will take a minute," Hans said.

"Where's your jacket?" the woman said.

The boy clutched his arms. "I don't know," he said.

The woman leaned forward and felt around the front seat.

"What's wrong?" Hans said.

"Have you seen his jacket?" the woman said.

"What color was it?"

The woman turned to the boy. "Answer the man."

"Blue," the boy said.

"Are you sure you brought it in the cab?" Hans said.

"It's my favorite jacket," the boy said.

The woman looked around the back seat. "It's not here," she said. "Stand up."

The boy struggled with the seat belt. The woman grabbed it from his hands and unbuckled it.

"You hurt my hand," the boy said.

"Maybe you left it at the house?" Hans said.

"Stand up," the woman said.

The boy stood in the seat, curving his neck to avoid the ceiling of the car. He stumbled forward in his seat when Hans stopped at the stoplight.

"Where's the jacket?" the woman said.

"I don't know," the boy said.

Hans reached for the meter on the dashboard. He nudged the glove compartment closed again.

"We're here," Hans said.

"Who told you to turn the meter off? Turn it on," the woman said.

"Why?" Hans said.

"Start it again. We're going home."

"I want Waffle Place," the boy said.

"You're not getting anything until we find your jacket."

Hans circled the parking lot and turned back toward the green house. He looked in the rearview mirror. The woman was mumbling to herself, loud enough for the boy to hear. The boy was crying. He made eye contact with Hans through the mirror. Hans focused on the road ahead. The boy stared at Hans every time he glanced at the rearview mirror.

"Drive faster. Stop milking the meter," the woman said.

Hans drove faster. He needed the jacket more than the boy needed waffles. Hans hoped one day the boy would understand.

———————————

Pardeep Toor grew up in Brampton, Ontario, and currently lives in Las Cruces, New Mexico. His writing has appeared in *Electric Literature* and the *Midwest Review* and is forthcoming in *Great River Review*.

EDITOR'S NOTE

Beneath a highway overpass, a high school boy hollers as a truck barrels by, feeling the vibrations in his body, straining to hear the sound of his own voice above the roar. "Salt" is a wonderfully sensory story, full of heat and sweat and physicality, and also quiet watchfulness. We follow Chava as he watches a boy named Fermín play goalie at an intramural futbol game on a sweltering day; talks with him for the first time at the rundown hotel where his family lives; and takes a field trip with him and other students to the strange Salton Sea in Southern California, where the water is drying up. One teacher describes the Salton Sea as "a big fish graveyard." Another says, "Few can survive these harsh conditions."

Alberto Reyes Morgan's sharp prose captures the numerous threats these boys face—violence, prejudice, deportation of family members. Amid these harsh conditions, desire delicately blooms. "Salt" renders concrete a private intensity that gathers inside and is almost too dangerous to express, even to oneself, and lays it bare in its stark, painful beauty.

Polly Rosenwaike, Fiction Editor
Michigan Quarterly Review

SALT

Alberto Reyes Morgan

JUST BEFORE SHE left forever to Sonora, my amá said she'd given me the tit when I was a little boy for longer than I needed. Not to have me stronger or healthier, but as a way to keep another pregnancy away. My apá believed in raising as many escuincles as God handed down for his two-bedroom apartment.

And that last time we were all still a family, while I stared at the cracked plastic of my amá's packed bag, she also open-handed me across the face on account of the dirt that I'd brought inside.

It had followed me from beneath the highway overpass. That tawny soil had caked my green backpack and the navy blue pants of my middle school uniform. Her slap never took, because I kept going beneath the overpass well into my high school years.

The sun didn't scorch under there. I would lean against the warm, but never burning, concrete walls, my lower half cushioned by the finely ground soil. When I heard the slow rumble of a large vehicle, my back tightened. As the vibrations grew stronger in the concrete and rolled into me, I looked at the sloppy E and L tags the Eastside Locos had sprayed on the wall. Jagged 13s in thick block letters with red drip lines that ran down and met the smooth soil.

I felt the vibrations coming down my body as a double semi was heading toward the México border just a few miles away. The shaking noise, the heavy rumble. My uncut nails clawed into my knees as I hollered at the trailer going past, trying to hear my own voice.

"YOUR PARENTS PROBABLY work outside, under this same sun, when it's even hotter," declared Mr. Borland, from beneath his wide-brimmed sombrero. We followed behind his lanky body as he swiftly led us to our high school's futbol field. That afternoon Mr. Borland, a trained athlete made to teach biology, gave us the bullet points of the scientific method. His sunglasses still on, he explained the importance of participating in the intramural matches he'd organized with some of the other teachers. He railed against soda and the fried food from the ice-cream truck. According to Mr. Borland, these twenty minutes of sport could change our lives, but most of us only watched.

Every few weeks I'd catch him at night, shirtless, running on the unlit streets toward my corner of town. He seemed to stretch taller as he galloped down the black asphalt, his white skin silver as his sweat caught the moon. I'd hear his pounding feet, the gasps of breath, as I walked home in the dark.

Today, in the August humidity, my bleached hair slicked back with number five gel for maximum lock and hold, I was all in black. A poor decision on my part, made exclusively because I'd read of the slimming properties of all black.

Straggling behind with me was Yisel. Her broad shoulders flabbed down into the fleshy edges of her wide back. A constellation of freckles covered her soft pink face. I didn't care that she'd tried multiple times to convert me to Christianity.

Rene Cruz came up behind her with his big gold chain and big jeans but surprisingly understated small diamond earring. In one motion, he put his hand over her lower back and squeezed her tight to his body. I didn't know she was into cholos.

A drop of sweat ran off my sideburn. It landed on the bare dirt of the futbol pitch. A dark spot that shriveled in seconds.

On the pitch, clouds of dust and dead golden grass rose as the ball was kicked around. A group of students watched the game; many hands raised over many eyes to block out the sun. In the confusion of moving bodies, I slinked away while Mr. Borland and another teacher struggled to put a team together for a match.

Though I saw people I knew, they weren't the kind I felt I could approach. In an attempt to shake my awkwardness, to look interesting yet disinterested, I took in my surroundings: The dead olive tree baked by sunlight, its cracked trunk filled with stashed knives and homemade foil pipes. Our rusted school fence. A light blue sky that stretched past the chatter and heads of the spectators. Across that sky lazed wisps of cloud fluff, which disappeared as they reached the bleached-white corona of the sun.

Suddenly, I heard a deep *boom* followed by a sharp *slap*. The ball spun up into the blue, while on the pitch the goalkeeper lay splayed faceup on the dirt. Dusty goggles strapped tight on his head hid his eyes from me. The crowd began to whistle and holler at what must have been a spectacular save.

Most goalies in these student games would, at most, halfheartedly stretch out a limp hand to make a save; the position was usually reserved for the girls who didn't want to get fussed up or the guys like myself whose technical abilities were limited. But as this goggled goalkeeper stood, the sun pouring down on him, I thought of an Aztec priest lifting a sacrificial heart for the sun.

He left alone the dirty brown patches on his creased navy blue pants and only spit into his hands, rubbing them together. He untucked his violet shirt—buttoned to the neck—and ran his fingers through his restless black hair. On top of his upper lip, a thin black mustache. I could hear his congested nose; he breathed like a short-snouted dog, taking powerful lungfuls of air. Standing in the crowd, as the sunlight slammed my body and I took the white heat, I watched only him.

He propelled himself into every ball. Arms stretched out, he ran shouting toward the strikers coming at him. The passion that ripped through his body moved in sheets of sweat through my own. Gluey lines of melted gel crusted on my cheeks and sweat ran down my shins, but I didn't care.

The drudgery of the desert dissipated. So, too, the repeating green rectangles of the agricultural fields that surrounded us. Those endless looped rows of alfalfa that speed past your car window, like some Hanna-Barbera cartoon background.

I STOOD BY the fence after school, marinating my clothes in my sweat. Cute girls waiting for rides hid their bodies from the sun in the shade of a lone palm tree. Round asses. Heavy chests. The long dark hair with touches of blond streaks. The narrowing waists, the widening hips.

An anxious energy filled me. At this point in September, my dad was still harvesting date plants out toward Yuma. My brothers weren't home either. Efra worked nights as a stocker at the Walmart and disappeared for most of the day. Chema was at federal prison for crossing into Calexico in a car filled with coke. He thought there were only bricks of weed in the tires. So nobody was home. I thought of going to sit in the cool shadow of the highway overpass to listen to the cars.

"Hey, Chava," a voice called out to me.

It was Luis Lozano, tall in an XXL white T-shirt draped over his bones like a tablecloth. I hadn't seen him in months, since before the summer break.

"Yo, what're you up to?" I asked.

"Just blazed a bit over at mota nation." He pointed behind him.

"You mean the alley with the couch and the car seat."

"Ah huevo! You know it. Just rollin' past to see who I see. Headin' to Fermín's cantón now. His jefita got mad last time I smoke there."

"Fermín?"

"You don't know him? You've probably seen him goalie here. Wears these funny goggles." Luis laughed by himself, his red eyes half-closed.

"Oh." Fermín, like the song by Almendra, with those soft cooed vocals.

"You're not doing shit. Cáele," he said.

Luis's head followed Lizbeth Treviño's ass as she walked past. She caught him, looked right at him. It pleased me to see his nervous eyes dart back toward me; he was just as afraid as I was.

On our walk to Fermín's house, heat radiated from the sky and reflected up from the cracked gray sidewalk. "So, you guys kick it a lot? What'd you say his name was?" I asked.

"Fermín. We play futbol at Zapata sometimes, at night. After the adults use up the daylight."

"The park past the tracas? At night? Don't the Eastsiders kick it there?"

"Yeah, but I'm cool with some of them. I kick it with El Papayo sometimes even."

"Didn't he shoot some guey in the head over there, a Westsider, no?" It seemed strange Luis would know those gueyes.

"Wasn't even like that," Luis said, and spit out through the gap in his two front teeth. "Just some guy from Chicali, not even from the Valley. Didn't even die."

It was even stranger to hear him defend them. He'd sometimes act hard, a real chingón. He'd tell me about his uncle Chito that lived up in Bakersfield, the big city. He ran a whole neighborhood up there.

But mostly, that all just seemed like talk. Over the phone, we'd laugh at cholos and their gangster leans. We'd kick it for days— sometimes beneath the overpass where he showed me how to smoke, how to hock a loogie. Then I wouldn't see him for weeks. He'd get suspended from school or wouldn't go. Then, middle of the night, between my apá's drunken snores, I'd hear a noise outside the big aluminum-foil-covered window of the living room. It'd be Luis, his skinny arm between the metal bars, tapping on the glass with his dirty wooden bowl.

We mostly watched Channel 5 rerun AAA matches all night. The commentators did the talking for us as we sat in near silence. I'd peek at Luis, his small eyes squinting in the television's changing light, the smell of wet fields coming off him with each bowl he packed. Other times, when a window rattle would scare me awake, I'd bend back a bit of foil but would find no Luis, only empty night.

A WARM BREEZE billowed Luis's T-shirt but did nothing to cool my burning neck. I struggled to keep up with his swift gait.

We walked on Main Street, away from the blocks of houses, dipping into the shade beneath the awnings of vacant businesses. Glass doors and windows displayed the empty insides of places like the Vacuum Shop, the Owl Cafe, Shaolin Five Animal Kung Fu. We passed a survivor, Julio's Marketa, a small convenience store where you could buy loose cigarettes, sitting in a city block all by itself surrounded by dirt.

"You still living with your tíos?" I asked Luis.

"Yeah, my cousins share the room with me."

"How is Neto? He still only playing Metallica on his guitar?"

"Oh, you didn't hear? He's not here anymore."

"What?"

"He got deported. He's in Chicali, can't get back."

"What the fuck! Guey, how'd they get him! At work?"

"No, the pendejo was kickin' it at the Circle K, by the house, you know. Went to go get a Choco Taco. Next thing, some migra asshole rolls up and asks him about his papers. Neto, being Neto, tells him he doesn't have any. So they took him."

"Verga. Out of nowhere."

"Looked too brown, I guess," Luis said, shaking his head. "He was always the most salado."

"You think at least he got to eat the Choco Taco?"

Luis pointed to a faded brown hotel I'd passed many times. "Right here."

"Here? In the hotel?"

"Around back."

I'd never thought of the two-story building that encompassed the corner of the block as a working hotel, though a sign jutting out of one of its walls designated it MAYAN HOTEL. Crusty vestiges of white paint clung to the splintered wood of the front door.

The back of the building faced a vacant lot covered in broken glass. There was a lonely brown door and a loud air conditioner hanging on to the window. As we came closer, the air conditioner's death rattle grew louder. But then I saw that it wasn't the AC unit making the racket. A chain wrapped around the poor machine and tied with a fat lock held it to the window. As it shook and buckled, the chain rubbed against its dull metal parts.

Luis knocked on the door, which scraped the floor and shrieked as it opened. There stood Fermín, his shirt unbuttoned, a white wifebeater pressed tight against his skin. He had chest hair that curled out the thin fabric. The unusual goggles were gone, replaced by a round pair of glasses that revealed the bushiness of his eyebrows.

"What up, cholos?" We slapped hands and my hand stung, but I felt the slap inside; my chest jumped.

"Fucking hot out here," he said through braces. "Come in, I'm Fermín."

"I'm Chava" was all I got out.

We entered a small yellow room and sat at a round plastic table covered in dishes and food. In the corner, on top of a speaker, stood a TV with bent bunny ears. The other end of the room was a kitchenette.

"I was preparing some churritos. You guys want some?"

"Sure," I said.

"Some water, too," said Luis.

Fermín grabbed three plastic cups from the table and filled each one carefully with a water jug sitting on the floor next to him.

Luis tilted back his head as he gulped down the water. *Glug, glug, glug.* His large Adam's apple danced.

"Bienvenidos at the Hotel Mayan!" Fermín said, standing and spreading his arms out wide.

"Cool house," I said.

Fermín shot me a smile full of metal.

Luis refilled his cup and said, "Those churritos sounded good."

Fermín pulled out a bag of green limes from the minifridge.

There were two rooms in the small space and in each I could see a twin bed. Neither bedroom had a door, just a narrow archway covered in cracked yellow paint. Yellow scabs of paint littered the dark wood floor.

"Your mom's cleaning?" said Luis.

"Yeah," answered Fermín, slicing limes into halves.

"What's she cleaning?" I asked.

"In the hotel. The rooms and stuff. But this house is separate, it's not connected."

Luis slapped the table. "Shit, if it was connected, Don Servín would be in here buggin' your mom all the fuckin' time! 'Señora Vázquez, recuerde el bleach. El bleach!' Your mom already hates him. She'd pour that shit in his eyes."

Fermín stopped slicing limes and laughed with Luis.

I didn't understand why that was so funny. Luis's old-man croak annoyed me, but Fermín laughed, so I did as well.

Fermín tore open a plastic bag of churritos and flipped a bottle of Salsa Amor into the bag. The brown pieces of hard, fried maíz turned red and softened and most of the salsa drained to the bottom, where a puddle of hot sauce marinated those last lucky pieces.

"Y tu papá? He also works in the hotel?" I asked Fermín.

He pinched shut the top of the churritos bag and shook it violently. "I don't have a dad," he said.

———

"Better that way," Luis said, rolling the plastic cup between his palms. "I met mine once. He's a real asshole. Fucking mamón," he said, looking at me. I never knew Luis had met his dad. "All he talked about was the Beatles."

"You told me about that," Fermín said. His fingers, with their small tufts of black hair near the knuckle, pinched hard into each lime, so that the liquid shot into the bag. He squeezed each one to its limit, until the last bits of pulp dribbled out. The juice ran down the insides of the bag and mixed with the pool of Salsa Amor on the bottom.

"Where did you meet him?" I asked Luis.

"At the Donut Avenue. The chinos sell good tea there, real sweet. My mom called my tía's house, thought I was old enough and should have a dad."

"He was in a shiny red car, right?" Fermín shook the churritos one final time and placed the open bag in the middle of the table.

"Yeah," Luis chuckled. He grabbed a handful of churritos. As he chewed, he sucked in cool air through his puckered lips and gave Fermín a nod of approval.

"Yeah, looked like a fuckin' joto in that Mustang," Luis said, still chewing. "Made me sit in it with him. Played that shit music with his system. Never got out of the car, just wanted to talk. Why the fuck would I want to talk with that pendejo. That's what I told my tía, anyway. She knew I was angry."

I was waiting for Fermín to grab some churritos first, but he looked at me and pointed to the bag. His dark eyes were intimidating, yet there was a gentleness in his attention.

I thought it'd be rude not to dig in, so I popped some into my mouth. The stimulation of spice and acidity made my mouth water.

Fermín had been waiting for me—he plopped a handful into his mouth. I noticed Luis's furrowed brow, a confused wrinkle between his narrow eyes.

He tossed his head back and continued, "I threw out the chicle wrapper he put his cell number on. Said he'd buy me my own cell, so we could talk. But fuck it, que se chingue."

Fermín chewed with his mouth open. His fine-trimmed moustache contrasted with the fullness of his lips. As his mouth chomped up and down, I saw that his braces were missing the wires. Silver jewels encrusted his teeth. Fermín maintained his gaze on Luis while he kept speaking, but I'd grown bored by Luis's bastardly rant.

"What I should have asked that puto, really, is why he doesn't fix up my mom's papers, you know? Why not do that? But, who knows . . ."

"My amá left too," I blurted, not entirely sure why. "Some years ago."

Luis and Fermín stared at me.

"Yeah, I know," Luis said. "No big deal right, ni pedo." He dropped the last few sopping wet churritos into his mouth. Those were the best ones.

The empty bag lay between us—a gutted animal—hot sauce and pulp leaking like viscera from its mangled plastic body. On the table, we spread our dangerous fingertips, wet with Salsa Amor and lime. Those red fingers, in a forgetful moment, could take their vengeance on your face or, for the most unfortunate, your cock.

I could feel the heat from our feast rising in my mouth.

"Too much Amor?" asked Fermín.

"Just the right amount," I answered.

Ms. McGaw held up a bottle of hand sanitizer and squirted a gelatinous dab into her open palm. The rubbing alcohol smell wafted toward me in the back of the minibus, then disappeared as the funk of manure blew in through the open windows.

"Would anybody care for some?" she asked. "A little goes a long way."

That morning we'd left the high school and traveled in two white minibuses to visit what Ms. McGaw called her "favorite ecological accident." We had no AC. On the highway, the roar from the open windows beat down all conversations and within minutes our excited chatter turned to silence. The plastic cover on my beige seat warmed and grabbed my flesh like wet glue.

North we went, across fields of crops and desert for what seemed hours, until in my groggy haze I saw the sign: SALTON SEA STATE RECREATION AREA. Past the decay of forgotten houses and rusted hulls of cars, the dark blue sea—its color found around here only in the sky—reached out wide in all directions. Behind the blue, the distant horizon jutted up as smooth caramel-colored mountains.

I'd seen the Salton Sea once before, when my cousin drove us past it on a camping trip. "It's really a lake," he said. "Mutants and religious locos live out here." Caifanes bumped in his car's speakers. "They eat the three-eyed fishes that fuck in that thing."

Once we were off the minibus, the Salton Sea welcomed us with a moist breeze that carried a hint of rot. Sticky sweat coated my bare skin.

Ms. McGaw stood in the sunshine and rubbed sunblock into her arms and face, but she didn't rub it in all the way. The skin on her arms looked even redder with the creamy stuff on them. On her face, the sunblock thickened into the creases of her wrinkles.

Suddenly Fermín walked up to Ms. McGaw. He wanted sunblock to protect his fair skin. No. It wasn't that. He'd gone to tell her to rub the excess sunblock further into her skin. Now she wouldn't look like a clown.

Fermín wore a red shirt, brown pants, and a black pair of dress shoes that shined. His tucked shirt showed off a white belt made of some kind of reptile.

I felt nauseated. Was it the putrid odor coming from this unnatural body of water? Death's smell? Ms. McGaw had told us the water was drying up, and as the Salton Sea died, dust storms would blow the lake bed—full of the poisons from our fields—back to our towns for our asthma-ridden lungs to breathe. She called it ironic.

I walked toward the water, white pebbles of who-the-fuck-knows-what crunching under my shoes. I kicked around a bit and uncovered the remains of a fish.

Ms. McGaw and Mr. Fillmore chatted as they walked together along the crunchy white shore and asked us to follow. In her raspy voice, Ms. McGaw explained that agricultural runoff kept the Salton Sea alive. That many types of birds visited, and if we were lucky . . .

I saw Fermín walking toward me. His black dress shoes were nearly gray now, completely covered in the white sand stuff of the Salton Sea.

"Yo, haven't seen you around," Fermín said. "You don't hang at Zapata?" He kept his voice low.

"Sometimes. I saw you, though, one of those games during first period. I forgot to say when Luis and me went to your spot last week. You were like a cat."

"Ni pedo. That was nothing. Just messing around."

"No, you were real good, bien cabrón."

"Now, follow along this path," Ms. McGaw said. The moist breeze picked up, carrying her words, as well as the water's stench, to us.

"Got no homies here?" Fermín asked.

"Nah, not 'students of promise,' I guess," I said, using air quotes.

"Don't make fun, guey. We were handpicked for this. Enjoy it. Only *we* get to see all of this," he said, spreading his arms out wide.

"You seen Luis lately?" I asked.

"A couple days ago, at Zapata. I goalied for his team. Says he starts at D.O. in a few weeks or something."

"Pinchi idiota. Rolls a blunt at school, then *has* to blaze in the library."

"Always bragged to me the dog would never catch him, that he was cool with Officer Peña. Didn't even matter." Fermín shook his head.

Mr. Fillmore tightened and adjusted his ponytail to cover his bald spot. "So," he clapped his hands once. "We're basically walking on top of a big fish graveyard. Those are fish bones that you're standing on."

"What!" cried some of the group, followed by "guacala" and "gross."

Fermín kicked a few of what I now knew to be bones onto my sneakers. I kicked some back at his shoes.

"See, now you'll have to clean these," he said.

"What, they were dirty as fuck, already all cochinos."

"You're crazy, I could see my face in my shoes."

"All right, I'll do yours, but you'll have to do mine."

"Sneakers are no thing, I'm wearing real leather."

"You look nice," I said.

Mr. Fillmore was much farther ahead now, though the crunch of his hiking boots was still audible to us. "That smell is dead fish. That sound, the bones of thousands of fish breaking," he said. "Hundreds of thousands, in fact."

"Millions," said Ms. McGaw, as she walked ahead of him.

I found myself at peace, surrounded by fish death. We were headed for a tall hill.

"You ever go into the hotel?" I said.

"A few times. Have you?"

"No, just your house."

"Yeah, my house. What the fuck, right?"

"Nah, what do you mean?"

"I mean, I live in a hotel, Chava. That doesn't seem kinda fucked to you?"

"Shit, I thought it was cool. Honestly. I mean, you probably get to be around some cool stuff."

"Yeah, I guess." He smiled. "There is this one veterano kinda lives there. About half of the people just live there."

"In the hotel?"

"Yeah. I see the same people all the time. This veterano's room is right above mine, my walls are like paper. So, this guy used to be real hard—"

"It's the salinity level of the Salton Sea that killed the fish we're standing on. Few can survive these harsh conditions," Ms. McGaw said.

Fermín continued, "Yeah, so this guy, Ernesto. Real barrio. He claims Chicali 13. One day he's walking through Posada del Sol, you know, the apartments by the Raspado's Toño."

"Don't really know the north side," I said.

"Then you don't know Raspado's Toño? Crazy. Guey, they hook it up there. They got so many different types of syrups you can use. They get so good that I eat too fast and feel like my brain's gonna split. But rico."

"A raspado would be good right now . . . So what happened with the guy, at Posada del Sol?"

"Right, so he starts going over there because his haina's there. Him and this girl go way back, he used to finger her in high school."

"You know all *that*?"

"He told me, talks more than a parrot. So, since his haina's at Posada, he starts to sling there, just mota, I think. Northside hears of this—"

"The tilapia is one of the types of fish that survives these waters," said Ms. McGaw.

Fermín leaned in close to me. Sweat rolled down and landed on his whiskers. "Posada del Sol has no lights. Ernesto is walking through and the Northsiders, they come up on him, and they got bats and paquetelas. They slam him till they drop him."

"Damn," I said.

"Kept going while he's dropped. He had to have metal plates stuck inside his head. You see him now, guey, his dome looks crazy. It doesn't make sense—bulges out here and there. It's the metal."

"Verga," I said.

"All right, guys. Walk up here, there's a great view. We'll be able to see a great variety of birdlife from this vantage point," Mr. Fillmore, on the hill, called out to us from behind a pair of binoculars.

"But here's the real chorizo of the story." Fermín's body pressed closer to mine, a hard shoulder against my soft flesh; his mouth moved close to my ear. "I hear him at night, when I'm in my bed. Never the same girl's voice. I hear smacking, like cachetadas. She's breathing hard, and slapping and slapping, and he shouts shit like 'Dale duro! Smack that head! Puro pinchi metal!' Sometimes the women stop, maybe they freak. But he orders them, like a veterano, and they always keep smacking him."

By the time he finished talking, white saliva crust lined the corners of Fermín's mouth. As we reached the top of the hill, my heart and eyes throbbed in unison. I became aware of how wet I was; my T-shirt was a moist rag stuck on my skin. Calm waves moved across the dark blue water of the Salton Sea; they flowed away from the skirts of the mountains and rolled to its shore.

"Look." Ms. McGaw pointed toward the mountains. "Those are pelicans flying over the water."

A black speck of a bug landed on Fermín's neck. Two trails of black hair ran down from his head, through his wet nape. I crushed the bug with a small slap that covered my palm in Fermín's sweat.

He turned toward me, those black eyes held wide—usually carefree, until they weren't. Now they looked only at me.

I showed him the dead insect in my wet hand, and that furry brow of his relaxed. He looked to the water. Ms. McGaw's white pelicans flew tight to the surface, crossed paths in an X shape and flew apart.

I brushed off the dead bug and moved my hand toward my mouth. I licked the sweat he'd left on my palm; the taste of his salt swam through me.

———

LUIS HELD HIS body like a lizard taking the sun. "See, fists down," he said, holding his naked torso over the hard cement. "The middle knuckles take all your weight. They're the ones you use when you punch some puto." He began a ferocious sequence of push-ups.

There was only a small nub of the sun left on the horizon. We were awash in the soft orange of the security lights behind an abandoned Kmart. I watched Luis's thin but firm frame sweat as he showed me how El Papayo had shown him how to strengthen his knuckles.

"So, this is your own personal gym then," I said.

He wouldn't stop to talk to me.

Finally, he stood. "The cops never roll through. We can smoke, work out, tag the walls, work out. Do some on your knuckles, go." He pointed to the cement.

"Nah, I don't think so."

"You're a bonbón, cabrón. You know las honeys, first thing they look at is your arms," Luis pumped his veiny arms up and down and began to do jumping jacks. "Or don't you care about girls?"

"You learn about that at Desert Oasis?" For a second I felt bad for mocking his continuation school, but he was acting out.

"Ha, D.O. Shit's a joke. You turn in a packet a week of bullshit and get out by noon. Stopped going. A month in I'm doing pericasos with Mr. Z in his trailer. Pure Colombian shit that gets flown in. He parties with El Papayo."

I wanted to leave. "Be careful with El Papayo. I keep hearing shit."

"Careful?" Luis said, as he stopped jumping to take gulps of air. He smirked and pulled out of the long pocket of his sagging gray Dickies what looked like a metal pipe with a handle and trigger on one end.

"I got my hechiza," said Luis, holding the crude weapon up proudly, his chest quickly rising and falling.

The homemade gun looked like it might only pop a pigeon's head off, but when he pointed it at my face and said, "What do you think? El Papayo said always keep her loaded," I nearly fell on my ass.

"Ya guey!" I shouted. "Point it away!"

He kept walking toward me, one corner of his mouth turned up, his quick shallow breathing, that shitty little pipe pointed at my head. I lost my cool. I wanted to cry. I ran and behind me saw Luis shouting from inside the orange fluorescence, "You gotta work your arms, mijo!"

BACK THEN, ZAPATA had no light at night. A few weeks after the trip to Salton Sea, Fermín had invited me to one of his matches. As the game ended, the sun was in its final descent. Slivers of cloud lined the sky and soaked the dying light, as if purple bruises had sprouted across it.

When it was finally black, Zapata emptied out. Fermín and I sat on a patch of grass beneath a mesquite tree in the park. Across the street from us was a dirt lot filled with torn-up tires. Houses stopped growing here, at the end of town.

Through the buzz of cicadas, I heard footsteps behind me. We turned and saw Luis walking toward us in the dark, shirtless, cigarette in hand.

"A bunch of us are going to Alex's house to drink. He got a chingo of Tecates left over from his sister's quince." The lit end of Luis's cigarette grew brighter as he sucked it down. The soft glow lit up his face and stretched out the menacing shadows of his cheekbones. "Or you guys staying here?" Luis asked, blowing out smoke.

"Yeah, just for a bit. I'll rest up my knee a bit, then head over," said Fermín.

I heard Luis wheeze as he walked away.

The stars appeared from behind the black clouds and more cicadas joined the chorus. The darkness of the empty lots behind Zapata stretched out so far that it became hard to tell where the ground and night sky met.

Fermín had his leg out. He rubbed his hairy knee with one hand. He'd dashed out of his box for a one-on-one, bravely dove into the feet of the striker, and kept the ball. But the man, and it was a man—Fermín played against full-grown adults—had jumped and landed on his knee. I could see the red cleat markings.

"What do you think, hang here or go to the kickback?" Fermín asked.

"Whatever's cool," I answered, hoping we'd be able to just talk by ourselves.

"Or we can stay until the chicharras stop buzzing. They're giving a real concert."

"Man, those things go all night. We'll never leave." An excitement I couldn't place in my body made me jittery.

"Yeah." Fermín looked down and ripped out a tuft of dry grass from the dirt.

We faced the empty railroad tracks. And though I never saw it, I imagined that the smooth steel of the tracks themselves must glow under a full moon and create a luminescent line that cut across the east side. But now there was only darkness—on the pitch next to us, in the sky over us, in Fermín's eyes behind his goggles.

"How'd you stop that guy? You're so focused out there," I said, pointing to where the action had taken place.

"You liked watching me out there?" Fermín took off his goggles and sweaty shirt, stuck them into the duffel bag at his side.

"Yeah, guey. But I wish I knew how you do it. How do you not care about these mamones yelling at you from the side, and everybody looking at you?"

He scratched his bare chest. His wet chest hair covered his fingers.

"I guess it's like you said, I focus. Then it's like nothing matters, not my mom, not school, and especially not these pendejos out here."

I didn't know when it began, but our mesquite tree now buzzed with cicadas. Fermín put on his round glasses as he looked at me.

I remember the sensation of a prickly pear cactus gently tapping my fleshy back as I pushed in to kiss him. And as the sharp taste of salt from his mouth and neck covered my tongue—the brackets on his teeth scratching my lips—I felt the coming sheets of sweat. This wasn't a lonely drop running down my chubby cheek; it was my body pumping its aquifer and pooling in every pore—from the arch of my nose to my damp shins.

Before he left, he wanted me to come along too but I refused. I worried he'd notice how nervous I'd become. I worried he'd touch me and become disgusted by my warm sweaty skin.

"Are you sure?" he asked.

He was so calm.

"I gotta get back. Date work ended some days ago, I think. My pop will bug out all loco if he shows up and no one's there," I said, swinging my arms in a way I'd never done.

"Mañana?" He smiled at me.

"Yeah. Tomorrow."

I shook as I watched him walk away, down toward the weak streetlights, to Alex's house, which was next to the park. I saw him go up on the bare wooden porch that all of the small houses there seemed to have.

It was the only time we kissed.

I should've gone with him.

THE NEXT AFTERNOON I walked to the highway overpass. I saw Luis, but he didn't holler back. He came up to me, too close, and asked, "You even gonna deny it?"

"What?" I couldn't take a proper breath. I knew.

Luis stuck his face out and said, "Hit me." I couldn't move my legs.

He gripped my bleached hair and used it like an anchor, pulling down until I was kneeling before him. He hammered my face over and over with the side of his fist until I heard the *crack* of my nose breaking. He let go. I flailed on the ground, reaching for something to stop the pain. I'd been smacked around plenty by my apá for not watering his neon-red bird's beak chiles. I'd let them wrinkle like an old woman's neck. This was different though; Luis needed to make a point.

As I crawled away from him, I noticed how the fine powdery soil beneath my face was caking into black globs from the blood gushing out my nose.

I could hear a voice. I hadn't realized Luis was talking to me. He wasn't yelling or anything.

"Stay the fuck down, maricón," he said. I could hear his feet pacing in the dirt behind me. "Shit's for your own good." It felt like he was talking to himself. I looked up, the crimson tags of *Es* and

Ls and 13s danced. My mouth tasted metallic and salty. My eyes
burned, sweat seeping into them.

"Fuck did I just say, hijo de tu puta madre!" The back of my
scalp stung, a fistful of my hair in Luis's hand again. Now he was
angry. Over and over, he rammed my face into the black dirt.

WHEN I WOKE I felt the coarse wall of the overpass, a warm can of
Coca-Cola in my hand. A group of middle schoolers in their uniforms were staring at me, their eyes like a tribe of goats.

"Hey! You got fucked up," one of them said.

"Tómale a la Coca," said another, in a hushed tone, as if he
didn't want to startle a monster.

My face throbbed and sipping the Coke made it hurt.

I needed to be far away, get to the apartment. I felt embarrassed,
but a kid helped me stand while the others watched and exclaimed
"damn" or "a la verga."

Every step was like Luis's hands on me again. I was afraid he,
or anybody, would see me so I tried to be quick. But the viejitas at
the senior living apartments were glaring at me. They sat inside the
small square of shade of their front porches, fanned themselves,
or swept the dirt that collected in the corners and knew. They
scratched at the flab of their brown sunburnt arms, aware of exactly what kind of person catches a beating like the one on my face.

At home, I sat and shook on the toilet, my wet underwear in my
hand.

OUR TOMORROW DIDN'T come. Fermín and I never had more than
a head nod between us. We understood the fear in each other's eyes.

The way I used to see him, as outside my reality, was gone. He was no longer part of another world, but instead rooted down by force into mine.

In a way, Fermín got lucky once Luis put out the word. When some Eastsiders jumped him at Zapata, they could have taken both eyes. It wasn't their mercy, I heard later, but his futbol goggles that saved his left eye.

IN THE MIDDLE of drives through the miles of crops, and into the death of the desert, he'll come to me—his goggles on his face, his tousled hair still holding black even after all the years. I hit the border, cross to Mexicali, have tacos al pastor, Chinese food, visit the cousins. Buy my insulin, turn back, always north to the USA, hours' worth of rows of cars waiting to cross beneath an angry sun. Migra officers that always ask—half paying attention—the same rhetorical question: "Why did you go to Mexico?"

And in my sweaty car I think of his young moustache, thin as if penciled in, styled like the men on my abuelo's worn trio records. His gentle black eyes; the burn of salt on my tongue.

Alberto Reyes Morgan hails from the Mexicali–Imperial Valley border region. His writings and translations have appeared in *Invisible Hands: Voices from the Global Economy*; *Underground America: Narratives of Undocumented Lives*; *Solito, Solita: Crossing Borders with Youth Refugees from Central America*; *Michigan Quarterly Review*; Texas Public Radio's *Book Public*; and other venues. A graduate of the MFA Program for Writers at Warren Wilson College, he has taught in Ethiopia and Spain.

EDITOR'S NOTE

"Re: Frankie" is so many things at once: a fabulously imaginative recon-struction of a literary classic, the zany epistolary of a hapless "waste" col-lector, an account of unrequited love and online harassment and men who can't (or won't) take a hint, and the women who endure them. But, in its illustration of sexism equal parts humdrum and horrible, "Re: Frankie" is also a story about how the banal can be fatal—a story that, in its depiction of a dystopia toward which we sometimes seem indubitably bound, asks an even more troubling question: Are we there already?

"Re: Frankie" represents that which we value most in fiction at *Porter House Review*: a new voice, a unique and incisive perspective on human ex-perience amid social dilemma, ambition in form and style. We are proud to have published it, and eager to see what Mackenzie McGee will come up with next.

Sam Downs, Fiction Editor
Porter House Review

RE: FRANKIE

Mackenzie McGee

Subject: CONSUMPTION WARNING

Dear Valued Customer,

We recently received a bill showing unusually frequent usage of your home ReJuve Total Self Regeneration™ Unit. In order for your ReJuve to continue producing the highest quality of care, it is crucial to limit your use to THREE CYCLES per seven-day period.

Here are some tips for preventing overuse:
- Consume a balanced diet and engage in regular exercise
- Avoid stimuli that may provoke a hysteric episode, such as excessively sentimental books, movies, music, and people
- Utilize less invasive Revitalization Technology, such as the DeepBreathe™ Oxygen Mask or DeepDive™ Bubble Bath
- After the onset of hysteria, wait one day before using your ReJuve, as hysteria may subside on its own

- Confirm that a hysteric episode is genuine by consulting the Quick Hysteria Questionnaire on the side of your ReJuve Unit

We at ReJuve are committed to women's health and well-being. Should you notice any repair or maintenance issues, please contact myself or another Biowaste Professional with details.

Sean Rasmussen
Biowaste Management

Subject: YOUR WASTE CYCLE IS CHANGING

Hi Julie,

Okay, so this isn't actually about your waste cycle, but I think the emails from my personal email are going to your junk folder or something, and I keep getting sent to voicemail every time I call. Anyway, your hairbrush is still at my place. It's the fancy one your sister bought you in Paris, the one with the boar's hair bristles and wood handle. It's a really nice brush.

Don't go back to that plastic brush I bought from Walgreens when you stayed over the first time. Remember how it pulled the knots down to the middle of your back, so you looked like the girl from *The Ring* with a bird's nest at the end of your hair? You joked that a family of owls was living in there and they were overdue on rent. You had to comb your hair with your fingers, and your hands smelled like coconut shampoo all night. Your hair was so long back then.

The brush is safe at my place. Let me know when you want to come get it.

Sean Rasmussen
Biowaste Management

Subject: Re: YOUR WASTE CYCLE IS CHANGING

Julie,

Listen, I'm sorry for tricking you with the whole fake-subject thing. But it looks like this is a *The Secret* situation (I finally finished the copy you gave me), because it's becoming true now. Your waste cycle *is* changing, so maybe it wasn't really a lie in the first place. My boss told me that Randy and I are switching our afternoon routes, so he'll be in charge of your waste from now on. He'll probably be late more often than not, because he likes to "take his time with the ladies." That's how he refers to them. Calls it respectful, the sentimental old man. He still uses individual body bags, if you can believe it.

My boss also told me the reason we're switching is because you specifically requested that you be put on another biowaste guy's route. I don't really know what to say, except that it would have been nice of you just to talk to me and not go to my boss behind my back.

You're the one who said we should stay friends, but I guess you changed your mind, and you didn't even have the decency to tell me to my face. Or respond to a single email, for that matter.

Sean Rasmussen
Biowaste Management

P.S. I still have that hairbrush.

Subject: Re: Re: YOUR WASTE CYCLE IS CHANGING

Hello Julie,

I just wanted to let you know that I'm heading over to your place because Randy asked me to. It's an issue with your rejuvenator unit. I swear I'm not stalking you, just helping out a friend.

Sean Rasmussen
Biowaste Management

Subject: THERE'S AN ISSUE WITH YOUR WASTE

Dear Valued Customer,

This message is to notify you that myself and a fellow waste professional (Randolph Olson) have discovered an issue with your ReJuve

Unit's ability to properly destabilize waste products. We strongly
advise you to SUSPEND USE OF YOUR UNIT until the issue can
be resolved.

If you experience a hysteric episode in the meantime, DO NOT
GO DIRECTLY TO A HOSPITAL. Instead call our complimen-
tary DeepDelphi™ Hotline at the number listed on the side of your
ReJuve Unit. A certified counselor will be available to discuss your
symptoms. If your counselor deems your hysteria valid, he will fill
out documentation certifying your state and forward it to your local emergency medical provider.

A repair team will be dispatched to your home in the next two days
during normal business hours. You do not need to be home during this time, as our professionals will be working solely with the
ReJuve Asphodel Meadows™ Waste Disposal Tank on the outside
of your home.

In case of any gate codes or dangerous animals on the property that
are not currently on file, please respond promptly to this email, or
call our local office at 952-XXX-XXXX.

Sean Rasmussen
Biowaste Management

Subject: Re: THERE'S AN ISSUE WITH YOUR WASTE

Julie,

This isn't an automated email. This is Sean. You need to call me ASAP. It's about your waste. Seriously, it's important.

Sean Rasmussen
Biowaste Management

Subject: Re: Re: THERE'S AN ISSUE WITH YOUR WASTE

Julie,

I don't give a shit if you block my phone number, my personal email, my goddamn good vibes, I'm gonna keep emailing you from Biowaste until you respond. This isn't about us.

Sean Rasmussen
Biowaste Management

Subject: Re: Re: Re: THERE'S AN ISSUE WITH YOUR WASTE

Julie,

Your waste is alive.

There, did that get your attention? Are you happy this is on my professional record? Randy called me to your place because your waste
was breathing and her eyes were open and everything.

Here's what happened. I had two units left when I got a call, and
I didn't answer, because I'm working on Working Hard On The
Task At Hand (you always told me I was easily distracted), but
then he called me again and again, and so I finally answered. I
said what do you want, I'm working hard on the task at hand,
and he was all choked up, like he was crying. I figured it must be
an old lady's unit or a little girl's unit, the kind of waste Randy
gets emotional about sometimes, and I was ahead of schedule, so I
went over to yours, and there it was. There were two other pieces
of waste, facedown and straight-backed, stacked up all neatly in
the order they were disposed, dead as they should be. Not dead—
deactivated. Except the one on top of the pile wasn't. Instead, it
was curled up in the fetal position on top of two other pieces.
This one, the most recent one, was looking around, all calm and
a little confused. Like it'd fallen asleep on a city bus and missed
its stop.

Randy said that we needed to bring it into the office and take care
of it. Then he started bawling like a baby because he hates the old
way of dealing with waste, he calls it inhumane (it's a damn good
thing he started after we got Asphodel attachments). He said he
couldn't put it in the trailer with the rest of the waste. I told him
to buck up and put it in the cab with him, but he blushed, said he
couldn't ride around with what looked like a bare-naked woman
sitting next to him, and besides, he'd already been written up before
for being late to drop-off too many times, so he told me to take it.

So here I am, arguing with a grown-ass man who's got tears freezing on his cheeks, stomping my feet to keep warm. The hatch to the Asphodel is wide open and your waste is looking around like an idiot, and Randy's looking around like an idiot, and I say why are you whipping your head back and forth like that, and he says he can't bear to look right at it, that it's not right, and I say it's not like you haven't seen a naked woman before, and he says I've never had waste look me in the eye and ask me what time it is before.

I look at your waste because I'm not a coward, and it's shivering. It's covered in goose bumps and it's got its knees pulled up to its chin and its arms wrapped around its legs, and it's got its face buried in the hair of the waste below it, like it's trying to keep warm. Randy yells at me not to touch it, but I do, and I jump a little when I make contact, but it feels just like normal skin, like your skin, maybe a little cooler because it was freezing out.

I'm not telling you this to freak you out. I'm telling you this because it's sitting in my living room wearing your old clothes and playing with your hairbrush, and it doesn't understand what's going on, and I didn't know who to tell about this, but I figured you'd want to know.

Sean Rasmussen
Biowaste Management

Subject: Re: Re: Re: Re: THERE'S AN ISSUE WITH YOUR WASTE

Julie,

I hope my last few emails didn't scare you. I promise that wasn't my intention. I figured, if my work is going to send you an automated message about me showing up to your place, I should tell you why, and if I'm going to do that, I should tell you what's really going on, and it turns out waste being lucid isn't as impossible as they made it seem in training. So I thought it was common courtesy to let you know what's going on. I'd do the same for any other customer.

Sean Rasmussen
Biowaste Management

Subject: Your Waste

Julie,

Once again, you were right—I'm just a grunt, a cog in a corporate machine, a serial number that clocks in and out and leeches off the company health insurance when my back acts up. What I'm saying is, it turns out that my superiors don't give a shit about my email, so long as I'm not forwarding spam or sending out nude pictures of

myself. Looks like it's safe for me to keep emailing you about your
waste, at least for now.

I told Randy I would go ahead and take her in to waste processing,
if he was going to be such a big baby about it, and that got him
all mad, but he wasn't about to take her in himself, so he said he'd
finish my route for me if I'd go ahead and do it. He took his coat
off, and then his sweatshirt off, and I said I don't know who you're
putting on a show for but I'm not interested. But he just took off his
flannel and gave it to me, and said to give it to her so she wouldn't
be cold at the end, she shouldn't be so cold. I said we're supposed to
use impersonal pronouns, and he said she's too much of a she to be
an it. I draped it around her shoulders, and she moved for the first
time, lifting her arms to pop the collar up around her neck. I turned
to ask Randy if he saw that. But he was halfway to his truck, he had
started walking away before he even put his layers back on. I swear
he was steaming in the cold.

I was going to bring her in. If paper jumped out of your shredder
at work, you wouldn't feel sorry for it. At least, that's what I told
myself. I thought, I guess Julie might feel sorry for her waste. You
could say it'd be easy for her to sympathize. But she'd also say it was
gross, it was biomedical waste, shit that didn't flush.

I was going to bring her in until we were on the highway, and we
were driving over the river. I kept looking over, to see what she was
doing, hoping I'd look and she'd be dead and I could just pull over
and throw her in the back. But as we got on the bridge, the trees
dropped below us and the winter sun was shining in the cab, and

she looked at me, and her face was red and her lips were puckered, because she was holding her breath, desperately trying to make it to the other side. She failed, like you, Julie, always do.

I swear I'm bringing her in on Monday. The incinerator is off all weekend anyway, and I think it'd be a little suspicious if they opened it up and saw a fleshy piece of waste blinking at them, sitting cross-legged on a pile of ashes. If you want to see her before then, let me know.

Sean Rasmussen
Biowaste Management

Subject: Re: Your Waste

Dear Julie,

I think I figured out why you're not responding. It would be too embarrassing for you to admit, which is why I'm not going to spell it out here. But rest assured—you're still the only Julie, the most beautiful Julie, in my eyes.

Sean Rasmussen
Biowaste Management

Subject: Re: Re: Your Waste

Julie,

Back in pre–Asphodel Tank days, the ReJuve was programmed to knock out wastes' brain waves, leaving them just there enough to walk and follow orders. They did this so we wouldn't have to chuck them one by one into the incinerator. They'd march right in, so long as we used a friendly tone.

During training, a doctor showed us two brain scans—the one on the left was all lit up, and the one on the right was almost totally dark, except for a few spots of color on each side. See how the right scan is all dark, the doctor said. That's what makes them waste. There's almost nothing there.

Another trainee raised his hand. But they still move and everything, he said. They still listen and talk. He cleared his throat and asked if they can't feel.

The doctor was ready for this question. Not in the same way you and I do, he said. When you're falling in a dream, you think there's momentum, you think the ground is getting closer and closer until finally you wake up with a start. Notice how you never landed. That's how they feel—like they're in a dream.

The trainee didn't like that answer much. He said, but they're still hysterical, aren't they, they're still the ladies they were before. Before is the operative word, said the doctor, annoyed. They're the ladies whose pain, because it was not visible to clinicians, wasn't taken seriously. The ReJuve system takes women's pain away, takes their pain seriously. Do you want it to be like the old days with hysterical women walking around in society, no one willing to listen or able to help? The doctor practically recited the answer. He probably got the question in every meeting with suits.

Until some suits got sentimental the way Randy did and demanded the Asphodel knock waste out cold. Before that, we talked about waste being dream-dark. This one's so dream-dark, I'd say. It'll barely move its feet. It's cutting into my lunch hour.

Your waste was dream-dark from the moment Randy and I saw her, to when she was riding in the truck, to when she was sitting like a statue in my living room, blinking and confused but still as a statue, holding your brush in her lap. She fell asleep around eleven, so I carried her to bed and tucked her in, and I was passed out on the couch when the lights flicked on. She was standing there in front of the TV, which was still on and playing infomercials for miracle shampoo, and her face was different, not calm and wide-eyed like a dream-dark waste's face should be. She stood straight, with that practiced posture you have, still except for her hands over her belly, grabbing at the air, like she had a bad stomachache. She was worried and lucid, and she asked me, in a scratchy voice, what time it was, and whether or not I was going to end it all.

Anyway, if you could come over and convince her that I didn't kidnap her and I'm not going to hurt her, that would be great. If she's as stubborn as you, you might be the only person in the whole world she'll listen to.

Sean Rasmussen
Biowaste Management

Subject: Re: Re: Re: Your Waste

Julie,

I really was going to take her in today. I had it written down, "Bring in Frankie," in the personal planner you bought me for Christmas. I'll admit it's the first time I've used it, but that was the only thing written on the page, so I knew I wouldn't have an excuse for forgetting.

We sort of had a fight last night. That sounds worse than it is. What I mean is, your waste wanted to leave, and I obviously couldn't let that happen, and so when she went for the door I grabbed her around the waist, and she punched me, but it was like being hit with little pillows, it was like nothing. I barricaded her in my bedroom, and she banged on the door all night, and when she stopped I wasn't sure if she'd just tired out or finally deactivated. But I opened the door and her hands were scraped raw, but there wasn't any blood, and I wondered if she had any blood, and then I realized that was a silly thing to wonder. She was crying and sitting on the ground. When I walked in, she lunged forward, and I tried to step out of the way, but she grabbed my leg, and I started to shake her off, but she just held tighter, and I noticed she wasn't trying to claw me with her nails (your biotin-strong nails), but she was hugging me, and trying to speak, but she couldn't make any words that made sense.

Remember last year, when we sat in the ER for six hours? When you were reeling, and they told you to rate the pain out of ten and you said it was an eleven? I told the doctor you don't act like that, not unless it's serious, but he just shrugged, asked if you were regularly hysterical, asked if it was cramps. It took them until the next morning to figure out you had an ovarian cyst. You'd been anti-ReJuve before that, asked me to quit my job and find something honest, but on the car ride home you asked me how much those ReJuve things cost anyway. I reminded you what you'd always said about those "Barbie machines," and you didn't say anything, but you gave me a look that made me feel like I'd been shot out of your solar system and I'd do anything to crawl back into it. When I opened the door, the look on her face was just like that.

Sean Rasmussen
Biowaste Management

Subject: Re: Re: Re: Re: Your Waste

I think she's fading on her own.

Sean Rasmussen
Biowaste Management

Subject: Re: Re: Re: Re: Re: Your Waste

Julie,

I keep thinking about how Randy said she shouldn't be cold in the end, and how we made each other promise that we wouldn't let the other die in a home or a hospital, and I think it'd be wrong to let her die in an incinerator. So right now she's bundled up in every blanket I own and she has tea (your fancy loose-leaf tea), but she hasn't drunk any yet.

Let me know if you want to see her. I have no idea how much longer she'll be around.

Sean Rasmussen
Biowaste Management

Subject: Re: Re: Re: Re: Re: Re: Your Waste

Dear Julie,

She's making words! I really thought the Asphodel Tank had
knocked her out, that she'd just have dream-feeling and that's why
she'd only ever babble and ask what time it is. I'd gotten used to
telling her the time every few minutes, just so she wouldn't get all
nervous and worried and riled up, and when I told her it was almost
2:30, she rolled her eyes and said I can read, and I thought I've
never been so happy to hear your cruel voice.

I keep asking her if she wants food or water or anything, but she
turns me down. She asks for tea, but she doesn't drink it, just holds
it in her hands, in the middle of her blanket nest like an egg. She
leans over to put her face in the steam. Once, I asked her if she
wanted to take a shower, and she turned around so fast she spilled
her tea, and she glared at me and told me I could shower by myself
before turning back around to watch *Green Acres*, and I was so
surprised I couldn't even correct her.

Before you ask—I haven't even tried to touch her.

Sean Rasmussen
Biowaste Management

Subject: Re: Re: Re: Re: Re: Re: Re: Your Waste

Dear Julie,

Okay, I did try to hold her hand, while we were watching TV on Sunday. She had both hands cupping her big mug of tea, as usual. Her right hand held the handle, but her left hand was a little looser on the side of the mug. I slipped two fingers between her left palm and the edge of the mug, which was crazy hot because the tea was fresh. Her hands had to have been burning. She didn't react. I waited for her to squeeze back, to push me away, to do anything, but all I got was nothing. The mug was too damn hot, so I had to pull away. I told her that's too hot, and she said I want it hot, I want to feel it. Her hands were pink, her palms red. Her face was white as a sheet, getting whiter as the day went on.

When I first saw her, and I picked her up out of the Asphodel Tank, I knew she was waste. I also felt that your soul was somehow still in her, that the ReJuve hadn't worked the way it was meant to. I even thought, What if this is the real Julie and the ReJuvenated one, the one that's walking around not in pain anymore, hasn't got a soul at all? It's silly, but it was real, it was in my bones, the feeling that she was real somehow, that at the very least this pain was making her real. That she wasn't you, but in some ways she was more you than whatever the ReJuve spit out when you used it.

She was fading, that much was clear. Even with all the blankets in the house, she was shivering. All she wanted to do was watch TV and sleep, but even when she was glued to the screen I could

flip between channels and she wouldn't react, didn't seem to notice if we were watching a gory horror movie or the evening news.
Normally, you would make a joke about not being able to tell the
difference between the two. She would blink.

I didn't have much time, so I asked her the question that had been
burning in my chest all weekend—why you hadn't responded to my
emails about the hairbrush.

She was more lucid in that moment than she had been in a while,
and she wasn't as real as you, but she was somehow more real than
you'd ever been to me. She talked like every word was important.

She told me her heart was acting up on Thursday night, that she
had been cleaning the bathroom for the third time that week to try
to make the nerves go away but they wouldn't leave, and I knew
she had bad nerves, and she had already gone for a four-mile run
and that usually helped to tire her out, and her heart rate had risen
at the peak of her run but had yet to fall, and so she came home
and drank a gallon of milk and started cleaning the bathroom and
nothing was helping, and she realized the milk she'd drunk was
my old whole milk, the stuff I'd used to bulk up and that it would
make her fat, that she couldn't run it off because she'd already gone
for a run that day, and all she wanted to do was take a shower in
her clean bathroom but she couldn't find her nice brush she used
when her hair was wet, and then she saw my emails about it being
at my house, and she knew in that moment that she'd either have
to use her ReJuve for the third day in a row or slit her wrists on the
kitchen floor, because nothing would make it stop except getting
out of her body. I knew she had a bad heart.

We watched a whole episode of *Hogan's Heroes* before I said anything. Then I told her she could have just come over to my place and gotten the hairbrush and taken the shower. She laughed, the sound like chimes, and I felt like a fool for thinking this had anything to do with me, and I felt like your soul was gone.

I'm taking her in tomorrow. I'll drop the hairbrush in your mailbox on my way home from work.

Sean Rasmussen
Biowaste Management

Subject: Frankie

Julie,

Don't worry, we haven't found another piece of live waste kicking around in your Asphodel Tank. And Frankie is gone. But now that Randy is your biowaste guy, I thought you should be aware of an incident I had with him last week.

I was getting ready to bring your waste in early, but it was below zero, so I went to start the car and let it warm up. I was scraping my windshield, reaching over to the middle where it's hard to reach, where you always made me scrape for you because stretching your arms out straight like that makes your coat slide up past your belly and your stomach touch the snow on the hood of your car. And it was biting cold, cold enough that I was too occupied to see Randy until he was right in front of me, standing with a baseball bat in his hand. I said what's that for, and he said it's to take care of the Frankenstein you've been harboring. Keep in mind, I hadn't told him squat about your waste. So I played it cool, said what are you talking about, and he said he still hadn't gotten his flannel back, that I hadn't even mentioned it, and he knew something was wrong, and he came by last night to ask for it back and saw me playing house with a monster.

I remembered the way she was at the end, how she woke up that morning and said I have to go now, and I said that's right, and she just said all right, let's get it over with.

I thought, boy that was strange, but to Randy I just said don't call her that. I told Randy she'll be dead in a few hours, and this broke him just a little, just enough to make him drop the act, and he said she's hysterical, she's just been in pain this whole time and I'm damn selfish for prolonging that. I said it's not like you to come over swinging a bat, what were you planning to do with it, and he sort of hunched over and said you ever see a hysterical woman, and I said I dated one for a year and her corpse for a weekend, and he said no I mean really hurting, doctor says it's true and everything. I said just once, when Julie had a cyst, and he said it's the hardest thing in the world, seeing your woman hurt and not being able to do anything about it, and I said the only thing harder has got to be living like that.

Then he got angry again and said you're crazy, you could lose your job over this, I ought to report you, and I said I know, and he said she's not really Julie, the real Julie is long gone, and I said I know, she won't answer any of my emails. He didn't have much to say after that.

I offered him a ride and he said okay, and we piled into my car, which was warm by then, with Frankie in it. Frankie is what Randy called her right after she walked into the incinerator. He said Frankie had bad nerves just like Julie. You could see her shaking like a leaf right up until the end.

Mackenzie McGee is a writer and poet. She is the recipient of a Walton Family Fellowship in fiction and a Lily Peter Fellowship in poetry. She is an MFA candidate at the University of Arkansas, where she is at work on her first novel. She lives in the Ozarks with her husband, the poet Landon McGee.

EDITOR'S NOTE

Here at *adda* magazine, whenever possible, we try to select pieces through themed open calls, taking on readers (often in various languages) and editors from around the world to help us out. All our submissions are read anonymously. Very occasionally we do offer special commissions to established writers; but, generally, we find open calls—ones free to enter—are the best way to find new voices and we're always delighted to learn a selected writer has never published before, such as in this case.

Mathapelo's powerful story came to us through an open call on climate change. From close to seven hundred entries, hers was one of only twenty selected. It was immediately apparent that she'd convincingly made, over the span of just a few pages, a small world of its own, a window into a world, in the way of all stories that stay with you.

JS Tennant, Editor

adda

THE STRONG-STRONG WINDS

Mathapelo Mofokeng

IN THE KITCHEN sits a cooler box. In it, a Fanta. The Fanta in the cooler box is not mine. Neither is it my grandmother Nkhono's.

It belongs to my father, Nkhono's fourth son. And today we will pour it over his grave to quench his thirst.

We were meant to visit him yesterday, but Nkhono said the weather wasn't good and the winds were too strong. I think she meant he'd enjoy it more on a boiling hot day like today.

It's always the same at Avalon Cemetery: the red sand, the unkempt weeds that Nkhono concerns herself with, the drinking fountain that promises no water, and the lump that sits in my throat. The walk is always quiet. Only the steady thud of the bag of Fanta bumping against my leg. The steady thud reminding me to snap out of it.

Plot A–H

"Surely something like this couldn't beat me," Nkhono says, her hand gesturing to a modest tombstone.

Nkhono hasn't been able to erect a tombstone for my father.

"It was never meant to be this way," she reminds me as we walk past the more elaborate tombstones. "He was meant to bury me."

Once God grants Nkhono some money, from the scratch card competitions, the lottery, or horse racing betting, I know she'll erect something decent for my father. For now, the rough plank above his grave will do.

It's always the same at Avalon, except today the cemetery is littered.

"It's the strong winds that yesterday brought," Nkhono says, as the gravediggers pick up the cigarette butts, beverage bottles, dirty diapers, food wrappers, and other litter with their shovels.

I'd rather the strong winds with their litter, I think. They're better than the strong-strong winds, which leave you picking up the pieces of your life.

We've had some of these strong-strong winds. So strong they destroyed the power line in our neighborhood. This is how our fridge stopped working. This is why we borrowed a cooler box. This is why a cooler box sits in the kitchen.

Plot I–M

Nkhono always insists on taking a water break at the drinking fountain that promises no water. It's also here where she eats her boiled eggs before taking her afternoon pills. The blue one for her bones, the yellow for her sugar, and the heart-shaped for her high blood pressure.

Nkhono says her sugar started during Mandela's presidency.

"Soon after his release," she'd say, "several trucks carrying bricks entered our townships, and after these more trucks arrived carrying sugar to stock the shopping malls that the bricks had built." But my aunt, Nkhono's firstborn, who tells me things young people shouldn't know, once told me that Nkhono's sugar started when Nkhono was pregnant with my father. Pregnancy-induced diabetes is how my aunt referred to it.

Nkhono offers me a sip of water before packing the bottle away. I decline because I have watched her mouth cover the entire edge of the bottle as she drank down her pills, and I cannot unsee what I have seen.

Nkhono's feet bulging through her sandals is another thing that I cannot unsee. I know we're halfway to my father when this starts to happen. I'll know we're closer when her feet start to slow down. I'll know we're closest when her feet start to drag, and I'll know we're there when her feet stand across a worn plank bearing my father's name.

Plot N

"Is this it?" I ask Nkhono as we stand across a heap of red sand.

"I think it is. Although without a plank, hard to say."

This is true. In Avalon rest hundreds of thousands of graves in different plots, each a grim tale. Plot A–H the story of a Black struggle for liberation; Plot I–M the story of a pandemic that took our neighbor away; and Plot N the story of a mother who can't find her son's grave.

"Let's start again," Nkhono says.

I watch her fragile feet maneuver the narrow path separating each grave, scrambling across the rocks as she retraces the steps we've taken during each visit.

Each attempt leads us to a different grave. Some with planks bearing the names of strangers. Others with no plank at all.

Nkhono has never had to take pills for her mind because she's sharp and always remembers to pack everything we need: a water bottle for the drinking fountain that promises no water; an empty bag for her eggshells; toilet paper for the exit toilet, which has none; and an umbrella to shield us from the sun on our walk home.

"Must be the strong winds that yesterday brought," she says. "The same winds that carried the litter must have swept the planks away."

Nkhono turns toward a different part of the graveyard, widening her search to encompass a different plot.

Plot O

A crowded funeral brings our search to a stop. We watch the coffin being lowered to the melodic singing of a congregation of women dressed in blue-and-white church uniforms.

I imagine it to be the funeral of an important person because the coffin is covered in our country's flag. Either that, or the deceased did well at showing face.

"This is why it is important to attend the funerals of others," Nkhono whispers to me.

She attends at least one funeral each weekend. Says it's important to show face at others' funerals, because when you die families will return the favor.

My father's funeral was empty and on his coffin lay my Sunday dress. Nkhono told me it was empty because my father didn't show face enough at funerals, but my aunt, who tells me things young people shouldn't know, disagrees, saying it was empty because people can't get off work on weekdays.

My father never attended church, though he always encouraged me to attend with his aunt, Nkhono's sister.

"Just to be safe," he'd say.

The Methodists also wear uniforms. A black skirt, white hat, and red blouse with five buttons. The buttons are a reminder of something I cannot remember, something that happened to Jesus five times.

Nkhono says church uniforms are a waste of money. But Nkhono's sister says church uniforms are important in order for differences in clothing to be hidden, so that the rich and poor can look the same. Makes me wonder why Avalon hasn't learned this—whether the graves of all deceased should be dressed with tombstones so that the rich and poor can look the same.

A backhoe interrupts, making the singing of the congregation faint against its beeping sounds.

It took a dozen gravediggers and me to cover my father's coffin. They scooped up the sand with their shovels and I with my hands. Repeatedly. Half-conscious until a belly of sand protruded from the spine of the grave. It should take only a few more scoops for the man on the backhoe to finish.

We watch the machine's long arm reach for the ground, tossing the sand into the burial hole until Nkhono jumps at the sight of a plank being dropped into the hole.

"Wait!" Nkhono yells, her voice drowning in the rattling metal of the backhoe. She pushes her way through the crowd and stands at the edge of the grave. "*Wait!*"

The engine stops. The singing dies. The weeping I hadn't noticed before now audible.

"My granddaughter and I have traveled from far to quench my son's thirst." Nkhono gestures at the bag of Fanta in my hand. "However, the plank that marks his grave seems to be missing and we have spent the afternoon searching for his grave."

The mourners shake their heads in sorrow, releasing long and heartfelt moans of despair.

"So what would you have us do, Ma?" yells a man I cannot see in the crowd.

The mourners gradually become quiet as they listen attentively to Nkhono.

"While the tractor was pouring sand into the grave, I noticed it pick up a plank and toss it into the hole . . ."

Silence.

"If only one of you could climb down into the hole and fetch the plank for me . . ."

Uproar.

"It would help me verify if it's my son's plank," Nkhono cries out.

"Quiet down, quiet down, believers!" the pastor interrupts, thrusting his walking stick in the air. I notice that the pastor's belly sags over his pants, and I wonder if he chose to wear a vertical-striped shirt to make himself look lean. "What does the word say, but to fear not anything and everything, including this harmless hole in the ground?" he says.

The pastor's words are met by respectful yet disapproving glances from the believers.

"Now which one of you will help this mother?" he asks.

"I'll fetch it," the backhoe driver says, climbing down from the vehicle.

With no delay he leaps into the hole. The congregation quickly closes in and looks over. The driver digs his hands into the sand, searching. He stops and pulls out the plank Nkhono saw, dusting it against his trousers.

I breathe short breaths, while Nkhono's only deepen and lengthen.

"Eh . . ." he says, glancing up from the hole, "the paint has rubbed away a little, Ma, but from what I can read, this person was born sometime August 1971, born again on 8 March 2019, and died 11 March 2019."

"Thank you," Nkhono says. "My son was born only once."

Empty Plot

We sit under a knobthorn tree on an open plot soon to be another letter of the alphabet. A gentle wind cools us down.

Nkhono speaks a great deal about the changes in the wind, measuring its frequency and intensity by the dust it leaves on the countertops. "When I was young," she often tells me as I routinely wipe down the counters, "one thorough dusting a week was enough." But my aunt, who tells me things young people shouldn't know, once pointed out that Nkhono speaks of the dust the winds have brought when she cannot speak of the grief the winds have caused.

As I rest my back against the bark looking across the open space, I wonder if one day this plot will tell the grim tale of even more lives taken by the strong-strong winds.

Nkhono's hands find themselves in the soil, unconsciously plucking at the weeds. She collects the weeds in the plastic bag with the eggshells. "Have you seen him?" she asks the ants that emerge from the soil. "A fourth deceased son? A man with an uneven hip, one leg shorter than the other?"

I remember wishing Papa would walk like the other fathers. That his limp wouldn't stand out as much. Even in his coffin he lay in a suit that fit one side better than the other.

"It's what makes me special," he would say.

Today I only wish that he would stand out. That something special would set him apart from the scattered heaps of sand with no plank.

THE CONGREGATION OF women in blue and white pass us. Their work is done. Not ours.

"Have you found the grave you were searching for, Ma?" a member asks.

"Not yet, my child," Nkhono says.

"You should inquire at the cemetery offices. They should be able to help you find it."

The congregation of women murmur in agreement.

"What time do they close and where do we find these offices?"

"At the entrance," she says, pointing to the gates of the cemetery, "but you can follow us there."

Nkhono opens her umbrella and shields us from the sun as we walk alongside the religious women. Some speak, while others chant hymns. Nkhono stopped attending church because she says the Methodists sing like goats. But my aunt, who tells me things young people shouldn't know, once said Nkhono doesn't attend church because church uniforms are reserved for first wives. And Nkhono, apparently, is a second wife.

A member walking next to me nudges my shoulder.

"Take," she says, handing me a box of some leftover Eet-Sum-Mors, "to have with that drink of yours."

I politely nod, though I know we won't because the Fanta in the bag is not ours.

We reach the exit of the cemetery.

"That room over there, Ma."

A member points to a mustard-colored room attached to the toilets by the exit. I always imagined the toilet paper to be kept in this room—stacks of toilet paper that someone has failed to carry over to the toilet.

"Speak to the man in charge," one member shouts.

"All he'll need is your son's surname!" a second cuts in.

"Mm, ask him for the grave number!" a third replies.

"Yes, from there you should find your son!" another adds.

"Good luck!" a final one concludes.

What I know is that all these women were simply showing face, because when it's your father or son you've just buried, you don't have much to add.

WE STAND AT the door of a cluttered small room. Nkhono softly knocks and a middle-aged man with a smirk on his face looks up from his desk.

"What can I help you with, Ma?" he asks.

"Good afternoon, my son. Eh, we are looking for the in-charge of this cemetery."

"I am the person in charge, Ma. Please, what can I help you with?"

"I'm here with regards to the strong winds from yesterday and the harm they have caused me."

"Did you lose a loved one?"

"No."

"Then what can I help you with?"

"The marker that stood above my son's grave has been carried away by the strong winds that yesterday brought, and we're here to request his grave number so we can locate him."

"Are you sure it was the wind? I don't recall it being that strong. Our trees are still in the ground and the roof to my office intact, so yesterday's winds were definitely not that strong."

I realize that perhaps it's not by its strength that Nkhono should refer to yesterday's wind but by its nerve.

"His grave was marked by a plank and, like many others', his has been blown away."

"The planks we supply were never meant to be a long-term fixture. Only a placeholder until families can erect something more permanent."

I wait for Nkhono to explain her unpreparedness—that mothers aren't supposed to bury their children—only she remains looking down.

"You actually caught me in the middle of working on some exciting new offers we have for our grievers."

He stands up from his chair while Nkhono and I settle across the table from him.

I place my father's Fanta on the table and Nkhono places the bag of weeds and cracked eggshells on her lap.

"For example, we've recently added a backhoe to our funeral cover, and soon we'll be offering white doves at funeral processions," he says, beating his hand against an empty cage on the wall. "We'll also offer a trumpet player and bottled water to quench the thirst of our grievers.

"Speaking of, may I?" he asks, pointing at the Fanta on the table. I expect Nkhono to say no, but again she chooses silence.

The in-charge pulls a tray of mugs from the tea station in the corner of his room. He places the stained mugs before us and reaches for the Fanta. I quickly shut my eyes, but the *fssst* I hear only confirms my fears. He pours some into each of our mugs, leaving the bottle empty.

"Now, mother," he says as he takes a sip, "what did you say your son's name was?"

By now I expect Nkhono to choose silence again, but she speaks.

"His name was Kelebogile Lehlohonolo Mokoena."

"And which year did he die?"

"Two, oh, one, six," Nkhono says as her finger traces a 2-O-1-6 in the air. "June," finger tracing a 9.

"Nine June 2016?"

"Yes," she says, her nod a beat behind.

The in-charge's eyes search through a stack of books below the dove cage. He blows off the dust to reveal labels on the spine of each.

"There you have it," he says, picking up a book so heavy you would think it carried the weight of each of the deceased bodies. He flicks through each page, his fingers scrolling through all the names.

"Mokoena, Mokoena, Mokoena," he murmurs, before his finger docks on one of them.

His eyes are hard to read, but I can read what's in the book. I can tell the Mokoena his finger rests on died the year I was born. I know this because it's written 2-0-0-7. But Nkhono cannot read this because she didn't go to school. She cannot even tell you the date she was born. Says back then, no one kept a good record of birth dates.

The same way the in-charge hasn't kept a good record of my father's burial date, it seems.

He searches through a new stack of books. This stack is placed on top of a dozen toilet rolls lined up in a row. He pulls out a book, beginning the process again.

"Mokoena, Mokoena, Mokoena," he murmurs, before his finger docks on another incorrect Mokoena.

"But you know, Ma," he says, his back to us as he searches through another stack, "these winds are only warning of the end days. The coming of Jehovah Jireh. My only question to humankind is: When will we start paying attention?"

He pulls out another book from the stack, beginning the same process we've watched him repeat countless times.

"Mokoena, Mokoena, Mokoena," he murmurs. "Ehe, here we go. Kelebogile Lehlohonolo Mokoena, 9 June 2016. Plot N, grave number KLM 993678."

Nkhono looks at me. I nod, reassuring her that I have noted the grave number in my head.

"Thank you," Nkhono says, as we stand from our chairs to leave.

"Any time Ma, but please, before you leave," he says, pushing the tray of Fanta closer to us, *"drink."*

————

Mathapelo Mofokeng is a writer from Johannesburg. In 2018 she completed an MA in scriptwriting at the London University of Goldsmiths, after being awarded the Chevening Scholarship. Her short films have screened at BFI Soul Connect, Underwire, London Shorts, and Aesthetica, among others. Her short story and essay publications include *adda*, *Popshot Quarterly*, and Goldsmiths Press. Mathapelo was long-listed for the 2021 Commonwealth Writers Short Story Prize, is currently working on her debut composite novel, *The Ministry of Sadness*.

EDITOR'S NOTE

We chose to publish Nishanth Injam's "The Math of Living" because it stood out as a memorable and unconventional story about an American immigrant's experience of family, nation, and loss. The careful precision and control of Injam's prose constructs a story of subtle but powerful emotional resonance. In his innovative integration of coding language into the story, Injam plays with the limitations of conceptual frameworks for dealing with complex emotional experiences.

Heidi Siegrist, Assistant Editor
Virginia Quarterly Review

THE MATH OF LIVING

Nishanth Injam

I'VE BEEN WORKING for the *Chicago Tribune* for about a year when it strikes me that I will go home in six months. The ticket has been booked, and I'm ready. My boss has reviewed the JavaScript code and made his updates for the day. The code is in production.

I'VE BEEN WORKING for the *Chicago Tribune* for about two years when it strikes me that I will go home again in five months. The ticket has been booked, and I'm ready. My boss has reviewed the JavaScript code and made his updates for the day. The code is in production.

I'VE BEEN WORKING for the *Chicago Tribune* for about four years when it strikes me that I will go home again in three months. The ticket has been booked, and I'm ready. My boss has reviewed the JavaScript code and made his updates for the day. The code is in production.

Everything about my going home is formulaic. Sometimes I

think this is my legacy—not everyone can write themselves a home. I tell myself it's the next best thing to being on a plane.

MATH OF LIVING [i] {

By the time this plane lands, I will have traveled for twenty-six hours.

This is not new to me.

The distance between the place I live and the place that lives in me is more than eight thousand miles.

Each hour of the journey home, I will look at my watch, even though the screen in front of me has a world clock. This is so I'm not fooled by the time zone changes. Each minute of the journey, I will have the consciousness of going home. I will try to forget it and involve myself in a good book. But there is no such thing as a good book when you are going home after [x] months. I can't but sense where the plane is heading.

The plane will land, and people will rise. There will be an extraordinary wait to get off the plane; men and women will argue about their place in the queue after retrieving bags stowed elsewhere. Then it will be over. I'll get through customs and exit the terminal. This is the moment I've been waiting for. My parents will be at the airport, waving at me from a sea of onlookers. They will be as excited as children. My father will do [a] or [b]. My mother will do [b] or [c] or [d]. It's not surprising that my parents will shower me with love. I know they cannot help it; they haven't seen me for a long time. They will offer to take my bag and ask [e] questions about my well-being. I will feel the weather greeting my skin. At this point, I haven't gotten into the cab yet, but I don't have to reach the house to know the conclusion of this journey. I've already walked through the door in that moment outside the terminal. Home is the recognition of the lives we led together once, the things that only we knew of. It is the sound of the river that runs in our veins. Or rather the shape of a story we tell ourselves. Who doesn't love a good river?

In the cab, my father will ask me either [f] or [g] before proceeding to tell me everything that has changed in the city since I last visited. My mother will ask [h] questions about the food I'd like to eat. I will enjoy this attention, this care that was missing when I was a child. It is also inevitable that [j] minutes later, my parents will start quarreling with each other. That is who they are, they cannot stop. I will start feeling anxious; I'll never be as happy as I am in the moment I arrive. The magic will be over, there will only be mundaneness left. I will briefly feel like rescheduling the return flight I have in [k] days and going back to work. But I cannot do that to my parents. Their faces are still glowing and I wonder if love is a candle lit by distance.

The cab will stop at the tollgate that keeps increasing its prices. My father will take out his purse, but he doesn't have [l] rupees. I will have to pay for the toll. He will not look at me, the humiliation in his face transforming into anger. My mother will glare at him, the shine entirely gone. This is not new; I know there is no money. I must continue to work, in a country that will never be mine, for them to have something to eat. Poverty isn't anyone's choice. Some lives are meant to be. There's a Hindi idiom for this I cannot remember. If language is a city, mine is crumbling block by block.

The flight attendant asks me if I want [m] or [o], they are no longer carrying [n], and I refuse it before I realize what I'm doing. I don't call her back. I'm sick of airline food. And then, of course, I cannot escape the guilt; I'm exercising a luxury I hadn't known before. I take consolation in the fact that I will enjoy sumptuous food at home. Everything will cost [p] times less. I'll have [q] rupees to splurge at restaurants. Better to go in the first few days, before the restaurant money goes toward our loan payments and household expenses instead. That is, if the medical bills don't take away more than [r] rupees. Everything is a calculation. My father has often said to me: Why are you spending [s] dollars on a plane ticket? Why are you coming home almost every year? As if I didn't factor this cost into the math of living. I remember telling him once that capitalism has figured out this shit. That having a day off makes a worker more productive in the long run. Just don't kill me over a plane ticket, I might have said. But you can never please the math teacher in a father, the one who taught you to solve for x first, before you do anything else. The things you say don't add up. There's no mathematical value to feeling adrift in a white country.

Seat belt warning: there is some turbulent weather. There are [t] babies on the plane, and they are all crying. I put on the headphones and pick a movie. One of the teenage lovers has cancer and has [u] months to live; I'm not interested. I ogle the house depicted in the movie; what I'd like is a spectacular home in which to die. I cannot stop working, I cannot abandon my people. My mother has severe bronchitis from years of exposure to heavily polluted air. I'd like to bring her to the country that has me by the collar, I'd like to say to my mother, "You gave me breath, and now, I want to help you breathe." None of that is possible without money. And time. And work. And exile. What has exile done? It has taken everything I had in return for the idea of a home far, far away. Home is the sound of a river you are better off keeping at a distance. What else can you do except listen?

There's a voice in the cabin telling me I am [v] hours away. I know how this goes; each flight is more or less the same. This is the part where I wonder if my father was right, if I should have stayed put in America. Guilt is what I have left after a lifetime of not acting on my desires. A rupee spent on a toffee is a rupee wasted, the ice cream that everyone is having is probably not good for me, *nothing* is always the correct response to *what do you want.*

In the cab, my parents will argue incessantly about the necessity of taking a cab. I cannot stand it; I will begin to wish I had saved the money and not flown home. We'll make do with [w], I'll assure them. My mother will cough from the dust creeping through the windows, and I will tell her I bought her American medicine, namely Tylenol, and she will smile. Anything foreign is good, and everything home is sickness. Haven't I been reading the news?

My father will ask me how I like America, now that I've lived there for [y] years. I will lie and tell him that I like being in a place of great freedom and opportunity. It's better to let him think of America as my future home, to let him float past all inconvenient truths. There's no reason to tell him that I will never have enough alphabet to build a room for myself.

The cab will stop at [z] traffic lights and I'll see change. The city that was once mine is no longer what it was; every street is altered. I will feel foreign to the city. If my parents do not come to the airport, if they are not alive, I will not know where I am. I might be in the same city, but I will no longer be home. I do not know what I'll be if I do not have a home to go to. I do not know what I'll do if I cannot see my experiences reflected in the eyes of someone I love. Home is where rivers die, letter by letter.

}

I'VE BEEN WORKING for the *Chicago Tribune* for about five years when it strikes me that I will go home in two months. The flight ticket has been booked, and I'm ready. The phone rings: my mother's lungs have collapsed. She is dead. The funeral is in two days.

My boss reviews the JavaScript code and makes his updates for the day.

The code is in production.

—————————

Nishanth Injam is a fiction writer from Telangana, India. He received an MFA from the University of Michigan's Helen Zell Writers' Program, where he is currently a Zell fellow. His work has appeared or is forthcoming in *Virginia Quarterly Review* and *The Georgia Review*.

EDITOR'S NOTE

What drew us to "Force, Mass, Acceleration" initially was the sheer ambition of its premise. It is a difficult thing to sustain a story when the reader knows its ending, doubly so when they know that ending will be the protagonist's death, but Heather Aruffo quickly seizes on the idea that the importance of Ana Mladić's story isn't in its ending but in its telling. With a deft blend of history and personal narrative, Aruffo carries the reader through Ana's twenty-three years of life, balancing her internal motivations with the history of the Balkans as it sifts through her and, of course, with Ana's slow realization of the horrifying actions of her war criminal father. It is a bold story deepened by its discussion of how those who are good to us are not necessarily good to others, one which I found myself turning over and over in my head long after reading. I am very glad that we had the honor of including it in *The Southern Review*, and even more glad that Heather Aruffo's writing will now find its way into the hands of even more readers.

Sacha Idell, Coeditor and Prose Editor
The Southern Review

FORCE, MASS, ACCELERATION

Heather Aruffo

On March 24, 1994, at the age of twenty-three, Ana Mladić shot herself in the head with one of her father's pistols. She found it in her father's study, in a cupboard in the Belgrade apartment where her parents lived.

You may not have heard of Ana, but you have probably heard of her father, Ratko, former commander of the Serbian army in Bosnia, who was responsible for the siege of Sarajevo and the Srebrenica massacre during the Yugoslav Wars. Of the great despots of the twentieth century, Stalin, Hitler, Mao, Ratko ranks among them. In 2017, he was found guilty of war crimes on one count of genocide and nine counts of crimes against humanity by the International Criminal Court in The Hague and sentenced to life in prison. No one had been tried for such crimes since the Nuremberg trials in 1946. Ratko firmly denies all of the charges.

But today, we will not speak of Ratko. Men, after all, have a way of swallowing the stories of the women in their lives. Instead, we will speak of Ana. I will try to imagine her.

In 1971, Ana is born in Skopje, which will later become the capital of North Macedonia. Her father is a platoon commander, her mother, Bosa, a housewife. Ana is their second child, their only girl. Her family has left Serbia for Skopje, where her father is stationed with the Yugoslav National Army. I imagine their lives: Ana's mother's face drawn and white as she holds Ana in her arms. Ana kicks and screams. Ratko leans down, draws the hair out of his wife's face, and takes Ana from her. He puts his hand on Bosa's shoulder. Ratko's father died when he was three years old, leading an attack against the Croatian fascist Ustaše in World War II. He vows he will never disappear for Ana as his father disappeared for him. He will never disappear for anyone.

Ana grows to be intelligent, kind, and quiet, with pretty dark hair cut like a bowl. Her mother has taught her to be polite, to cross her legs when she sits, to ask nicely for things she wants. She walks from the apartment block where she lives with her family in Skopje to school. She wears a uniform, a pleated skirt. Her socks come up to her knees. Around her neck is a red scarf. In school she sits quietly, absorbing every word. She has a mind that is ravenous, that seeks to consume everything it is offered. She wonders if that is something that other people realize. Her father is finishing his military training in the Yugoslav People's Army, recently promoted to lieutenant. He has proven himself to be good at leadership, at war making. Yugoslavia, he vows, will never forget his name. When Ana comes home, he pulls her into a crushing embrace. He is glad to see her. She is his little angel. Ana leans into Ratko. She imagines she can disappear into her father's chest, that it is a cocoon enveloping her. She looks up and smiles at his broad face, how much she loves him.

In 1980, Josip Tito dies. Ana is nine; her family watches the funeral on the television screen, the procession of his coffin, the lines and lines of state dignitaries who attend. Beside Ana, her mother hangs her head and cries, blowing her nose in a handkerchief. Her father sits on the other side of her brother, Darko, who squirms while watching the procession. Her father has a hard look on his face. Tito is like a grandfather to Ana, to all children. His picture sits above the blackboard in schoolhouses all across the country, smiling down with benevolence. He is the great leader of Yugoslavia, who liberated his people from the Nazis, who guided a middle way between the West and the Soviet Union. The slogan under which he has led his people is "Brotherhood and Unity," no one nationality greater than the other. For years, he has led his people with his fist closed, like the grip of a cruel headmaster. There remains the question: Who will succeed him?

When she is eighteen, Ana wins a place in medical school. She wants to become a doctor, and in Yugoslavia's heavily regulated education system, only the best students are allowed to attend. All her life she has been diligent, taken her notes and minded her equations, tied her red scarf straight. Her father is very proud; he likes the idea of his daughter becoming a medical doctor. It is only the beginning; perhaps his descendants will be more than the peasantry, more than soldiers. They are the Serbs; they will be the new rulers of Yugoslavia. In her first week of school, Ana follows a doctor in a white coat and the rest of her medical school class down the stairs to the basement. They are in a white climate-controlled room. Vacuum pumps shudder as they suck away the spent air; the room seems as though it is breathing. Inside, cadavers lie supine on metal lab tables designed for dissection. The doctor removes a pair of forceps from the cabinet, a pair of large scissors, a scalpel, a bone saw. "This is what you will use," he says. "It is impossible to understand the human body without first taking it apart." Around Ana, the other students are watching. The cadavers lie clean on their metal beds, covered in white sheets. They seem to be sleeping. Ana stares at them. She has never been confronted with death so close to her; to see a body is something different. When the doctor removes the sheet, the scent of formaldehyde overtakes her. The body is clean, devoid of blood and color. In death, it no longer seems human. Never before has she seen anything like it. She stares and stares; she cannot take her eyes away from it.

It is the year 1989. Yugoslavia is about to collapse, like an old man with congestive heart failure. Its ankles have swollen; its breathing is shallow. It sits down on a park bench to rest, leans back, looks at the blue sky, knows it will not get up again. In the years since Tito's death, Yugoslavia has begun to fracture. Old nationalist leanings flare again. Slovenia demands independence, then Croatia. On the six hundredth anniversary of the Serbs' defeat by the Ottoman Empire, Slobodan Milošević, the head of the Serbian Communist Party, promises unity for the Serbian people, who have been so long oppressed by their enemies. The Serbs have adopted a new constitution. With the death of Tito, everyone again is Bosnian, Serb, and Croat; Catholic, and Muslim, and Orthodox. The country is plunged into chaos. By 1992, it has collapsed.

In her first year of medical school, Ana learns physics. The way the equations on the board describe reality fascinates her. A vacuum is a space in which there is no air. The force of an object is determined by multiplying together its mass and acceleration. These concepts are applied in medical school. A vacuum can be used to aspirate spittle from the throat of someone choking on their own vomit. A bullet expelled from a pistol or a rifle moves with the velocity of the acceleration multiplied by the distance of the barrel. When it strikes its target, the force of the impact is the mass of the bullet multiplied by its acceleration. The same applies to someone caught in an automobile accident. This is a grisly calculus, used to determine causes of death, essential in trauma situations and in postmortem evaluations. In her exams, Ana calculates the force upon impact. From an M95/M24 rifle with a 57mm cartridge fired by a partisan; from a revolver, with a cartridge size of 3.57mm; from a semiautomatic, military issue, with a 9mm cartridge. From the Yugoslav People's Army, a standard-issue rifle, with a 7.92mm cartridge. Some of the bullets tumble through the body, coming out far away from where they entered; others explode and divert like birdshot. Each delivers a great force, with calculations too complicated to carry out regularly. They do not change the reality of the patient on the table, the steps that must be taken to salvage them.

As Ana continues in medical school, what is left of Yugoslavia festers. Tanks roll into Slovenia; bombs are dropped on Dubrovnik. Slobodan Milošević orders military police to stop opposition protests in the center of Belgrade. New countries bud off from the side of what is left of Yugoslavia. According to Television Belgrade, Albanians, Slovenes, Croats are all enemies of the Serbian people. But in the cadaver lab, Ana is insulated from noise. She has a distaste for politics. She is a medical student; she has her own important duties to attend. In the white room she stands, wearing a pair of white gloves, a mask over her face. In her hands, she holds a scalpel. Slowly, delicately, she incises the skin; blood beads like a water droplet. The smell of death, of preservation, is overbearing. Below her the cadaver stares up with blank, lidded eyes, as round as a child's marbles. It is a young man, who died from a heart defect. He is perhaps twenty years old, no older than Ana. All around the room, the cadavers lie on their gurneys. An old woman with snow-white hair, a man in upper middle age whose side is disfigured by leprosy. Bosnian, Bosniak, Croat, Serb, it is impossible to know in the basement of the medical school. No one knows where the cadavers come from. It does not matter, Ana thinks, death has come to gather each of them. She breathes in through her mouth. She knows that a greater concentration of CO_2 in the bloodstream will dilate her blood vessels, to prevent fainting and vomiting. There are another few weeks of the course and before the end of it, she and her classmates must finish taking the bodies apart. She must finish before she can move on to the clinic. The cadaver lab is an end she must survive. She takes a breath to steady her hand. This time, she tells herself, her nerve will not slip away from her.

In school, Ana meets a man. His name is Goran, and he is twenty-four, close in age to Ana, a member of her medical school class. He is handsome; on his days off, he wears a leather jacket, rolls his own cigarettes, bitterly reads western newspapers. He is the kind of Renaissance man who can manage science and humanities, theory and practice. He goes to protests in the center of Belgrade; he does not agree with Serbian nationalism or with Slobodan Milošević. When he was a child, his father was arrested for opposing Tito; it was a very hard time for his family. But things have never been, to his knowledge, difficult for Ana. He rather enjoys parts of Ana: her good looks; her soft, gentle spirit; her smile; the way she works hard, keeps her head down, defers to him in conversation. The way she is just demure enough to let him talk over her, but still strong enough to wield a bone saw. The parts of her he does not like are her naïvety, the way sometimes he believes he is speaking to a child. He tries to speak to Ana about politics, about the issues of their time, what to do about religious freedom, self-determination, but she never gives him her opinion; she has been trained not to. He sees her as a pediatrician, or a gynecologist. She tries to tell him, gently, that she would like to do trauma. Ana loves Goran very much. He is strong and intelligent, with a quick mind that she likes. He has a different, stronger way of seeing that Ana has never encountered before. She wishes she could be as intelligent, as independent as him. Someday, she tells him, she would like them to have a family together. Goran does not reply.

Ana is a top student in the medical school. She passes her pre-clinical coursework with top marks. When she receives the results of her examination, she brings the papers home to her father. He has been transferred now, from Pristina to Knin, in Croatia, to lead the Yugoslav People's Army against the Croatian National Guard. They are defending the Serbian Autonomous State of Krajina, Serbs in Croatia who have created their own autonomous republic. When she shows him the results he embraces her, smiles, and kisses her cheek. He tells Bosa to buy more meat from the butcher and opens a bottle of rakija. He takes much pleasure in his daughter's accomplishments; they are befitting of a Serbian family

of their status. These are his victories, as much as hers; it is only
natural that Ana would excel in her own battlefield, as much as he
does in his own.

In 1992, Ana begins her clinical coursework during the siege
of Sarajevo. A city known for its unity, as a place where Serbs,
Muslims, and Croats have lived together for half a millennium,
Sarajevo has always been a city of pride in the Balkans. Bosnia
has declared its independence; after a murder at a wedding in
Belgrade, there are concerns that an independent Bosnia will not
be safe for its Serbian population. Ana sees the first newspaper
reports on her way to the hospital for her first rotation: Serbian
paramilitaries taking up sniper positions from the tops of buildings, mortars firing from a police station, a barricade ringed with
concertina wire set up in the middle of the city. A medical student
Ana's age, a Muslim girl from Dubrovnik, is shot in the chest
crossing the Vrbanja Bridge. Ana throws herself into the clinics,
where she sees men, women, and children. Rheumy eyes, scraped
knees, broken arms, pregnancies. Many of the people in the clinic
are refugees, Serbs from Croatia, Bosnia, Kosovo, escaping violence. In the evenings, Ana spends her time in the cadaver lab. It
is a kind of meditation, to take bodies apart, to see why they are
broken. She has become obsessed with the origin of things, with
pathology, with sickness. The beginnings of a cancer, an infec-
tion, a disease. At the front, Sarajevo is locked in from all sides
to keep the location safe for ethnic Serbs. On her way between
the hospitals and the cadaver lab, she sees newspaper pictures of
tanks and gray-fronted buildings. The number of casualties is tele-
graphed across the front of the newspaper. The UN, she hears,
has been dispatched. She wills herself to ignore it. Her father is

out at the front, busy all the time. On the streets of Belgrade, he is heralded as the great defender of the Serbs. When he comes home and she is off shift, they relax and play Battleship together. He always lets her win. But in the cadaver lab, she is her own. The more bodies she takes apart, she thinks, the better she will understand them. In the clinic, she misses the sheer, tense reality of gristle, of muscle, of sinew, of bone. Slowly, she picks up the bone saw, secures the head in front of her. She puts the blade down, she slices. The blade shaves a snowfall of bone dust. The room is white and quiet, save for the whirring of the saw. The doctor who supervises her sits behind, watching. There is no blood; these bodies are no longer living. Ana holds her face and hands steady as a sheet; they no longer shake. She has been practicing how to anesthetize herself to this process of cutting and opening; soon it will be replaced by healing.

Goran rotates in the emergency room. He is tired. The shifts stretch over twelve, twenty-four hours; he exists on cups of black coffee, on shouting attending doctors, on ringing phones. The fluorescent lights, the smell of antiseptic has seeped into the pores of his skin. He does not know his hands from the metal ends of instruments. Every day, the airlifts come to Belgrade with the injured from the siege of Sarajevo. Soldiers from the Yugoslav People's Army, covered in sheets, their legs and arms wrapped in tourniquets, their fingers and toes white. His attending tweezes out slugs while Goran carefully unravels bandages. The bodies in triage are marked with colored tags. Green, yellow, red, black. Ana's father is their commander. He hears of the hospitals in Sarajevo treating their wounded by candlelight, without antibiotics or blood transfusions. Some have even had to amputate without anesthetic. A barbaric practice, Goran thinks; medicine has slipped back fifty years. Goran sees a man with gangrene, with black fingers, the coil of his intestines. Slowly, he attempts to suture them back together with coarse, black thread. He wonders what has become of the injured civilians, if they hide together with their doctors and nurses in the dark of the hospital basement, listening for mortars. He wonders what has happened to those who are not Serbs. In his mind's eye, he sees Ana's face, then Ratko's. Every day, he grows angrier with her; he feels she has caused this.

Outside of Sarajevo, Ratko Mladić stands in a field. He has ordered his soldiers to use their largest mortars on the city. Behind him, concrete buildings rise. Their windows have been blown out in jagged edges. They begin to look like faces. It is winter. In the field, it is cold, and snow clings to the tops of dead grasses. He raises his hands. "Shoot the raw meat!" he shouts. He laughs. It is the same way he has shown his son, Darko, to shoot sparrows. The target must be spotted through the sights. The sights must be aligned immediately below the target. The rifle must be carefully seated in the shoulder to avoid the recoil force. He laughs as his men shoot at retreating soldiers and cowering civilians. It is the power to choose who lives and who dies that interests him. He has become a modern-day liberator; Miloš Obilić, the hero who killed the Turkish sultan in Serbian legend. He watches as the bodies pile next to each other. Blood stains their shirts. Allah cannot save them, he thinks, God cannot save them. Only me.

Ana goes to Moscow for a conference. Her father does not want her to go, but her mother argues for her to have a place. "Let her go to Moscow," Bosa says. "It is all she wants." Ratko sulks, relents, and leaves. Ana kisses Bosa on the head and goes up the stairs to pack her bags. How glad she is for her mother. She goes to Moscow with Goran and other medical students. They walk across Red Square, look at pickled Lenin. The Kremlin is a fierce fortress; the red stars on the top of its spires wink in the fading light. The sun sets below St. Basil's Cathedral; rays glance off colored domes. GUM, Moscow's State Department Store, is illuminated in thousands of tiny pinprick lights. Ana and Goran trip over cobblestones, watch goose-stepping soldiers. Ana is content; she slumps against Goran. Goran is anxious. He rolls and chain-smokes cigarettes as they walk. One by one, the ashes and the papers and the filters drop on the ground. His hands shake. He becomes snippy with Ana. Every day, he hears stories of Mladić: Mladić the general in charge of the siege of Sarajevo, the man ordering squads of soldiers to wipe out entire towns of Bosniaks, Bosnia's Muslim population. Mladić, the Butcher of Bosnia. In Moscow, Ana stares at the television in the lobby of the hotel where they are staying for the conference. They beam up pictures of her father. She cannot believe it; she cannot think of her father in any other way than as her protector, the protector of all Serbs. The father she loves. All of it must be slander. All of it must be made up. Goran can no longer allow her willing disbelief. He finds her vile. "What other Ratko Mladić would it be?" he shouts.

When they return to Belgrade, Goran is finished. "You need to speak with your father," Goran says. "Or I will not love you."

Ana turns and looks at him. The cobblestones outside of the medical school are rough underneath her feet. In the distance, the bells of tramcars clang together. He does not know what it is like. Just as she struggles to deliver bad news to a patient in the clinic, so she cannot tell such a thing to her father. She cannot bear it. "I can't," she says. "Last night he was being so kind. He is always so kind. He called me his little angel." Her father was only back for a short while; she did not want to upset him. This she knows: she loves her father. She cannot imagine that he is the same man the newspapers and the televisions say he is.

Goran is relentless. With someone like Ana who has been so coddled, with no responsibilities, a person who can remain so willfully ignorant, he must be. She appears like a child to him, whose stability, whose livelihood, has been built on the bodies of thousands. Every time he looks at Ana, that is all Goran can see, Ratko, the face like a piece of gray meat, the olive-green uniform. "You can't accept that you've been raised by a war criminal," he says.

Ana stands, silent. She is desperate to keep Goran, even if she does not know why. It is better to have him than to have nothing. "No, I will," she says. The concession to Goran, to herself, seems like enough.

The next week, when Ratko returns from the front, Ana goes to speak with him. He sits outside, on the balcony of the flat in Belgrade. She walks through his study. His pistols sit in their glass case. Outside, red-tiled rooftops rise, studded by the bare branches of trees. He rises when she comes and kisses her on the head. She tells him she has seen his face on television, that people are saying he is responsible for terrible things. "I don't know what to think," she says. She tells him that she is going to quit her studies and become a nurse on the front, to draw her own conclusions. She will wear camouflage and ferry patients on stretchers across uneven fields. Noble, but as she says it, she wonders if her patients will find any refuge with her, in a woman with the name Mladić.

"My diligent girl, you would never quit your studies," her father says. He smiles and kisses her, as though he thinks she is joking. She doesn't move; it is the same smile she has seen on the television, in the newspaper pictures. The expressionless face, like a piece of gray meat. The bulky uniform, the thick forearms, the strange half smile, half grimace, as though he is beyond reproach. It is true, she realizes, all of it. Her father is responsible for monstrous things.

She does not tell Goran, for a night, for a week, until finally she agrees to meet him. When she tells Goran, he won't be swayed. He cannot imagine Ana speaking to Ratko or becoming a nurse. She has always been one for consistency, for following rules. "You know you wouldn't," he says. "You wouldn't dare. You never do." Ana stands across from him silently. Her father's voice echoes inside her head: "My diligent girl, my little angel." It is the way that her father dismisses her, that Goran has just dismissed her, which removes the air from her lungs. She cannot comprehend why they will not believe her, that they will not give her a chance, that they will not have faith in her decisions. "You don't know how hard it is," she says.

In the picture I find of Ana, she is pretty. She has dark hair, cut short, a heart-shaped face. She wears a red scoop-neck shirt with long sleeves. It is a family picnic; she is with her mother and father. They are outside. One arm loops around her father's shoulders. She smiles.

It is evening. Ana enters her father's study. She wonders how she could have been so naïve, how she could not have realized. She wonders if her father, or Goran, has ever loved her for who she is: a woman who asks questions, a woman who forges her own path. Outside of the window, pink light spreads across the sky of Belgrade, behind the gray blocks of apartment buildings. It is pink as tissue, like the inside of gums, like healthy intestines. Ana's face is red; she has been crying. The night before, she fought with Goran. He shouted at her, called her terrible things. On the side of the room, up against the wall, is a glass case. Inside are three pistols, given to her father by the Yugoslav military, for distinguished service. She removes his favorite pistol and looks at the inlaid panel, the smooth barrel, the hard-edged trigger. Life has become a closed-off corridor with no doors or windows, a ceiling that is ever lowering, walls that are ever coming closer together. It is crushing her, and she is no longer able to escape, either by running or by refusing to see it. At either end of the corridor are the men, Goran and her father, on the opposite ends of the same spectrum. She sees no choice. She kneels down, she swallows. She is a brave woman, she has dissected a cadaver, she has seen trauma patients, she has become numb to death, but to be faced with her own, that is a different story. But she is not brave enough for confronting Goran, for confronting her father, for living with his crimes. She cocks the safety, presses the muzzle of the pistol to her temple. She pulls the trigger; the bullet accelerates.

We do not know who found Ana, maybe Darko or Bosa. It is impossible to wade through the theatrics of Ratko's grief to the truth. Whatever it was that they found, I imagine blood and bone and brain, splattered across the walls, stuck to the ceiling. The thin wall of the skull at the temple would have aided with this. When the gun was fired, the force from the bullet would have been so great it killed her instantly.

Ratko Mladić rages and sobs. As soon as his son calls him, he returns from the front. In the morgue, Ana is laid out on a white sheet on a steel gurney. The morticians do not want to show him her body, because of the condition of her head. Her father sobs, collapses next to the gurney. Dried blood the color of rust blots the sheet. He has demanded to see her body. After so much death, so much killing, he has found himself unprepared for this.

At home, Ratko is angry. His boots pound up the stairs, as if in an ambush. He pulls all of his wife's bone china out of the cupboard and smashes it against the tile floor. He demands that they return to the coroner's. It must be a mistake, an elaborate political conspiracy, his enemies turned against him. They have killed his daughter. It is impossible that she has killed herself. In the kitchen, his wife sobs, her head on the table. He opens the door, shouts at her to be quiet and then slams it again. He is angry with Bosa, angry with himself, but he will never admit that. How could she have allowed Ana to do such a thing? He returns to the barracks, to the scent of dirty straw, leather, and spent gunpowder. He orders his troops to another exercise, makes them run and run until it is evening. It is where he has always belonged.

After all, he has always loved his family only so much as they have loved him.

In the apartment blood splatters the walls, the ceiling. It will take forever to clean; perhaps it will never be clean. Bosa does not go into the room; they have hired someone to do the cleaning. She has given up. She sits with her head in her hands at the kitchen window. Yellow light streams through it. She begs Ratko to allow them to move out of the apartment in Belgrade to somewhere else, where she does not see her daughter at every turn, in every room, where she does not walk in the stupor of misery. Soon, she and her husband will be on the run to the countryside, but they cannot know this yet.

In the trauma room, Ana angles the scalpel. It is her first surgery. She has graduated from medical school, moved on to her training to become a trauma surgeon, a future that will never exist. The attending stands behind her, blue gloved, blue gowned. All of the surgical team seems suspended; their gowns hang like the robes of angels. Ana looks down at the patient in front of her. She angles the scalpel, makes her first incision, parting curtains of pink dermis, yellow adipose, down to the shimmer of white bone. She slices again and hits an artery. Blood rolls down her cheek. No matter how she has trained herself, she has failed.

One year later, Ratko Mladić stands in Srebrenica. He has just returned from rounds, handing out candy to children. "Not one hair on your heads will be harmed," he says, holding up fat sausage fingers, "not one." He pats the heads of young boys. He is careful to watch while the cameras are rolling. They are shut off.

He gestures to his men and the waiting trucks. There is where they will load them. From the back of his own truck, he looks out over the houses, the roads, the fields, at the people held in circles. Men, women, children. How unjust it is that each of them is able to live, he thinks. They are Muslims, the great oppressors of the Serbs. To breathe the air, to smell the earth, when his Ana is dead. He holds up his hand. "Leave none of them alive," he says to his troops. Ratko sits in the truck, his hand on the side of his pistol. His troops gather men in a field and shoot them as they run. When the bullets hit the men, they drop like sacks of potatoes. In the air, a metallic scent rises.

What remains to be known is Ratko. Here, I have tried to imagine him, but no amount of imagination can change the facts. The collapsed bodies, the torn hair, the faces with the noses and lips and ears cut off. Faces blown to pieces from the force of the bullets' acceleration. Eight thousand sons and daughters, lain unceremoniously, one on top of the other.

After he is found guilty, Ratko Mladić is taken to Scheveningen prison in the Netherlands. He stares out the barred window of his cell and watches the ball of the sun fall behind the concrete walls. Before leaving Serbia, his last request was to see his daughter's grave. He always left her flowers; who will leave them now? He wonders about shaving razors and support beams, about ties and belts and capsules of cyanide. He wonders if he will see his Ana again. The bells of The Hague ring, closing out the evening, one more in the endless span of a life sentence in prison. This much he knows is certain: like the men in the field, he, too, will die.

Heather Aruffo holds an ScB in chemistry from Brown University and an MFA in fiction from the University of Alaska, Fairbanks. She is an alumna of the Tin House Writer's Workshop and has received support from StoryKnife. Her work has appeared in *The Southern Review* and *The Laurel Review*. She lives in Anchorage, Alaska, and works as a regulatory medical writer.

EDITOR'S NOTE

Isaac Hughes Green's "The First Time I Said It" impressed us immediately with its engaging narrative voice, rich character development, wit, and insight. We did not know at the outset that the story was a debut, and due to the long lead time of our print publication, we did not know when considering it that the horrific murder of George Floyd would bring activism against anti-Black racism to the forefront of our national discourse. Today's conversations are in no way new to Black Americans, of course, as Green shows us through the memories of his young, unnamed protagonist in this coming-of-age story that reflects on the narrator's run-ins with the most notorious racist slur in the English language. While exploring "the pain and the connectedness" the narrator feels as a Black person, Green also memorably portrays an individual character navigating family, identity, ambition, and growing up. We are thrilled to see Green's work honored with the Robert J. Dau Prize and look forward to watching this talented writer's career unfold.

C. J. Bartunek, Managing Editor
The Georgia Review

THE FIRST TIME I SAID IT

Isaac Hughes Green

I HAD BEEN out on the court for a hot minute. I'd woken up around noon, had a bacon, egg, and cheese from the bodega downstairs from my apartment, headed to Tompkins, and started working in. The summer sun blazed down on New York City—its heat thick like the bacon grease Dad used to save in cans next to the stove, or thick like Anna who sat behind me in history class and wrote our initials with a heart around them on the corner of my notebook, or thick like my hair when I'd tried to freeform it that summer after Afropunk. I'd won a few games that morning but lost more, so instead of being on the court sweating, I was on the sidelines stealing glances at the lifeguard on the deck of the tiny pool between the courts and the Zen garden. Eventually I got hungry again. So I walked to the pizza shop on the corner of Tenth and Avenue A. I got my usual chicken, bacon, and ranch slice with a healthy addition of red pepper flakes and Parmesan. Then I took it back to the courts and sat down and started to eat. I was halfway through the slice when I heard someone calling out to me.

"You wanna run?" asked a dude who looked kind of like Bo Jackson in his Nike ads.

I looked around.

"Me?" I said, thinking of the game I had just lost and the slice

173

I'd just paid for. I was a transplant to New York, which meant I'd never be called to play just because I knew someone. The court was always full of strangers.

"Yeah. You."

I got up. I looked him in the face to see if I recognized him. Maybe he'd been sitting on the sidelines when I'd dunked for the first time a few weeks before. Maybe he'd seen that game where I drilled four three-pointers and had just as many assists on those overgrown high schoolers the summer prior. Maybe he was the kind of guy who didn't pick his team based on who'd been winning and who'd been losing. Maybe he was an altruist who just wanted to see everyone have a good time. I tossed my slice in the trash and got up off of the park bench.

"Wait," he said while looking over at another player on the other side of the court. I looked over too and saw another guy who was a little taller than I am. I'd been tall up until about my junior year of college—the tallest one at our family gatherings. Then all of my little cousins had a simultaneous growth spurt. They sprouted up past my 6'1" to NBA-worthy 6'4"s and 6'5"s. And I was left looking up at them at the Christmas party, wondering if those special shoes that added an inch were really as undetectable as the advertisements said they were.

"I think we're good," the guy in the tank top said.

I looked over at the piece of pizza I'd thrown away in order to walk onto the court. I looked at the young man who'd picked me, then dropped me. I looked at his girl sitting on the sideline. I walked toward him until I was close enough to see the beads of perspiration shining on his forehead and shoulders. My heart sped up. My veins throbbed in my arms and neck.

I'd never said it before.

I mean, sure I'd cussed people out. But this was something different. The level of disrespect I'd been shown merited that special word. The one that conveyed the pain and the connectedness. The one that said I wasn't having it with this affront to the fledgling sense of self I'd been piecing together against great opposition since little.

As I worked up the nerve to say the word for the first time, the most significant times I'd heard it said before flashed through my mind like a parade of bikers past the hookah spot on a Thursday night or like the emotions I'd had for those White girls in college who started talking about how they'd fucked a drug dealer a few weeks before me right after we were finished.

I WAS BORN in Durham, North Carolina, but I grew up in a safe, sheltered environment—the kind that the Fresh Prince was thrust into after he said goodbye to his moms and made it to Bel-Air— in the suburbs of Virginia just outside of Richmond. We had four bedrooms and an oak bandstand out back. A record-label executive had used the house as a summer getaway before we'd moved in. It was a refuge for us too. But somehow the word permeated the walls that my parents tried to build around our family. As I got older I heard it used on street corners, at the YMCA summer camps and church youth groups that my parents made me go to, and in popular music. To me and to my family it was a reminder that even if we had enough money to eat at restaurants whenever we wanted or to go for rides down the James River in my father's boat, we could still be brought down to a summation of what we looked like and what people thought of us in two short syllables. And so we didn't use it. But that didn't mean it wasn't out there waiting to be turned on us.

I was ten years old and I was in somebody's barn with a hoe in my hand. There was rusted farm equipment everywhere. We'd passed signs that marked where slaves had been whipped and by whom, which I made sure to point out to my teachers as they casually walked by. They called it a field trip, but it felt like torture. After an entire unit on slavery and the great inequities it had enacted on the African American community, my fifth-grade class had been shipped out to some former plantation and asked to till the fields like a couple of us would have in olden times.

I said, "No."

"It's just an exercise," Mrs. Martha replied.

"Look, Jazmine is doing it," Mrs. Peggy chimed in.

I swallowed my pride and went out into that field. I could hear mother earth calling out to me. Reminding me like my parents had during Kwanzaa and Juneteenth that my ancestors would be proud to see me getting my education. Reminding me that I was their wildest dreams made manifest. Reminding me, like Grandpa did, that sometimes the cotton grew up high where he and the rest of my ancestors could pick it without bending over, and sometimes mighty storms allowed my ancestors to stay inside for the day and share stories about where they'd come from and who their people had been.

I raised that hoe and no sooner than I did, did I hear "You just don't want to do it because you're a nigger!" come from Brittany McCourty's mouth.

"Me?" I asked.

I was one of two Black kids in my class—the other of whom was across the way making short work of an imaginary row of cotton with a smile on her face—but it still surprised me to hear myself referred to that way.

"My dad said that there are good black people who want to get jobs and be a part of society and there are niggers who just want to lay around and live off of other people's hard work."

"You're not supposed to be using that word," I said.

"Maybe if you weren't acting like one I wouldn't have to."

I cried then, quietly and to myself. My tears fell from my cheeks and stained the reddish-brown soil below as my hands worked it into neat rows and columns like so many men and women before me. I thought about speaking up, and then I felt a hand on my shoulder.

"We want to talk to you about something," Mrs. Martha said.

"It's okay," I replied. "I don't want to make a big deal about it."

"Well, it's a little too late for that. You can't walk around using the B-word toward people and expecting nothing to happen."

"I didn't say that."

"Brittany McCourty said you did."

"I didn't call her that."

"What happened?"

"I don't want to talk about it."

"Is it because you said something you shouldn't have?"

"No."

Mrs. Martha cocked her head to the side.

"We're going to have a talk about this when we get back to school. I won't tolerate profanity, and I certainly won't tolerate lying about using it."

"I just want to go home."

"You will. And your mother will be waiting to speak to you about what you did today."

It turned out that she was. And she wasn't happy. Neither of us were.

I MOVED AWAY from the predominantly White town I spent my early childhood in and came back to my home state of North Carolina. We were moving back to a community with roots in Black culture and entrepreneurship. It's what the family needed. At least that's what my dad told people when they asked him. His hair was graying and he was becoming overweight, which I thought was a natural part of growing older. In reality it was probably due to the stress of supporting a family, raising a "spirited" child who wanted to be an artist when he grew up, and hitting a glass ceiling. Hard. Toward the end of our time in Virginia, I overheard strained conversations during which he spoke in his White voice to defend himself from his bosses at his finance job. I didn't understand all of the words he was using. But where he used to laugh and joke, he now sounded like he'd rather be talking to anybody else—like he'd taken it as far as it was going to go. Later on, when people asked and he started spouting off a spiel about how Durham had been the home of the world's greatest Black-owned firm and that he'd always wanted to start his own business, I stayed quiet or gave him the benefit of the doubt or some combination of the two.

Uncle Jimmy died. Then Grandpa died too.

I watched my father try to hold it together as I grew older—old enough to realize that's what he was doing. My parents still tried to protect me by enrolling me in private schools and settling in another White neighborhood. But my father made sure I knew I was Black in small doses of unchecked realness that never ceased to surprise and amaze me. One day we were driving on Old Chapel Hill Road. We passed a branch of the old Black-owned bank that had helped my father start his company and the Blue Cross and

Blue Shield building. Oaks and pine trees lined the streets. We got into a turning lane by the gas station on the corner—the one that had the cats that liked to jump from the pork rind shelf onto cases of Budweiser. Who knows what was going through his mind. Maybe he'd been having trouble keeping up with car payments on the Mercedes we were riding in and wanted to prepare me in case we had to make some changes. Maybe he missed his brother and his father and hoped I'd be able to help him fill the void. He played NWA for me. "Real Niggaz Don't Die" off of *Efil4zaggin* a.k.a. *Niggaz4Life*:

Die, nigga! We are born to die, nigga
You've been dyin' for four hundred years

He turned down the music for a second and then looked at me.
"Remember, son. You my number one nigga on the trigga."
I smiled.
It wasn't how he usually spoke— Black voice or White one. But it still felt genuine. Even coming from a financial analyst. I could see his struggle and my own, and somehow, that word bridged the gap.

I WAS EIGHTEEN. I had saved up a little bit of money and moved out of the house and onto a friend's couch back in Virginia. I was trying everything I could to be independent but didn't really know how to do it. After overstaying my welcome at my friend's place, I started camping out in hotels and libraries. Eventually I bought an RV to live in and got ripped off by the seller and then a mechanic once it broke down. I decided to take the train to Durham just before

Thanksgiving. And I got into a disagreement with my parents on the way. They yelled through the phone that I needed to get my college degree.

"You need structure! It's fine to want to be an artist, but you need to go through the proper channels!" my mother said through my cell phone's tinny speaker as the Amtrak *Carolinian* I was riding on made its way through Rocky Mount.

"It's a side hustle," my dad added. "Name your favorite artist, and I bet I could look them up and find out what their day job used to be."

I ended up staying in yet another hotel—a discount one, because I was running out of money—about a mile or so away from my parents' house. The first night I was there, I went outside to have a cigarette. As I was walking toward the exit door, I could hear what sounded like a house party from one of the rooms nearby—men's voices rapping to Tech N9ne and the sound and smell of bottles of beer. It seemed a little dicey, so I decided to stay the course and head outside.

The heavy metal door closed behind me as I took a Marlboro Light out of a white-and-gold packet and lit it between my fingers. I thought back to when I used to steal those same white-and-gold packs from my mother's purse and glove compartment when I was younger. I wouldn't ever smoke them back then. I'd just throw them away. It hurt me to see her hurting herself. And if I'd had a mirror, I suspect it would have hurt me to see the look in my own eyes at that exact moment too.

I wanted to be the big homie.

I wanted to be looked up to.

I wanted people to hear about me before they saw me.

And I never for a second thought twice about the fact that all of those things were more important to me than actually creating anything worth looking at.

The door squeaked as a man about my own size and build walked out of the hotel hallway into the empty parking lot I was standing in and asked for one of my cigarettes. He leaned on the railing next to me and placed it in his mouth.

"You got a light?"

"Yeah." I handed my lighter to him.

"What you doing out here?" he asked.

"Just handling some business."

"Where are you from?"

"I'm *from* here," I said, my eyes narrowed, my disposition wary.

"Oh, you're *from* here," he said in a voice that mocked the concerned tone in my reply.

"Yeah," I replied.

"Then what are you doing staying at a hotel?"

"I-It's hard to explain."

"Can't be."

"I don't always get along with my parents."

"Oh. Okay. I've met young guys like you before. A few of them are back inside the room with my brother right now."

"What are you all doing?"

"You really want to know?"

I said nothing.

"Wait here. I'll go get them."

The man disappeared through the door. I waited outside in that empty and secluded parking lot, even though something was telling me to leave. All of a sudden the door burst open. The music was loud from the hotel room as people began to empty out of it. In a flash, I was flanked by twenty men in various shades of

Black—African Black, High Yellow, Mixed, and Part-Red. They all followed and took their cues from one man among them who was the tallest and best looking. He wore a neon-green shirt, a gold chain, and a devious smile.

"This young man told me he's having a disagreement with his parents. Told me that's why he's staying at this hotel," the guy I'd given a cigarette to said to the taller one.

"I don't know. You didn't mention he was so skinny," the taller guy replied.

"Who the fuck are you?" I asked impatiently.

"I'm Will. This is my brother. These are my employees."

"What kind of work do you guys do?"

"Construction when we can get it."

"What about when you can't?"

"You already worried about that? We haven't even offered you a job yet."

"I didn't know you were going to."

"Well, you have to earn the offer."

"By doing what?"

I looked around and realized that all twenty of the workers' eyes were on me.

"Maybe we don't need everybody," the smaller brother said.

"You're right," the bigger brother said. He waved his hand and ten or so of the men went inside.

"Do you have any skills?"

"I make art on my computer."

"Right. But practical ones."

"No."

"Well, we can start you off well above minimum wage. We'll give you a check that's better than any you've ever had before. Ask any of my guys," he said before turning to the ones left. "You all just started with me and your check hasn't ever been better, has it?"

"Yeah," they said in a disheartened tone. Their clothes were shabby. Their shoulders were thrown forward and their gazes were piercing. I thought back to stories I'd heard from my cousins about people who were jumped into gangs and exploited. My fists clenched as I sized them all up.

"I appreciate the offer," I said. "But I'm about to go to New York."

"Nigga," the taller brother said. "You don't understand."

"What don't I understand?!" I asked as I thought to myself about how the way he used the word was both familiar and threatening.

The men laughed to themselves.

"You can't just be out here dolo."

"I'm *from* here," I said.

"Yeah, he *from* here," the shorter brother mocked me again.

I could see the taller brother getting frustrated. The sinister smile that had crossed his face during our entire interaction was giving way.

"What's in New York?" the taller brother asked.

"I'm gonna go to school," I said. "Art school."

"He's got dreams," the taller brother said in a half-mocking, half-serious tone. He patted me on the shoulder, and I could sense that I was off the hook for whatever I'd been on the hook for before.

I GOT A portfolio together and applied like my life was on the line. Soon afterward I was admitted to Pratt. After convincing both of my parents that I could learn how to make money doing what I loved by getting an arts degree, I moved to Brooklyn and made an honest attempt at doing so. Sophomore year rolled around, and I moved into what had once been a sweatshop. The building had been converted into loft spaces where young artists lived as many as five or six to a room. The apartment I moved into had wood floors and a big common space with bay windows and a heater that hung from the ceiling and sounded like a low-flying plane when you started it up in the winter. I'd found the place on Craigslist. When the landlord had taken me to see the unit, the tenant had yelled at him for not scheduling the visit first. But the space was huge, and when I brought a few of the friends I'd made in art school to see it we all agreed it would be a great idea to move in.

One was from Connecticut. He was a model and a photographer. He rolled his own cigarettes from a blue bag of tobacco and painted when he wasn't shooting or writing in his tiny brown notebooks. Another had introduced me to the model. He was one of the first people I met at Pratt and was a friend who was slowly becoming a rival, because we were competing for the same people's attention and the same school-sponsored grants. The third was a shy girl from France. Once we were living together we began to have parties, and we had so much space that we could host bands and upward of a hundred people at a time.

I spent some time around my model roommate's friends. They were a privileged and uniformly White group. Most of them kept to themselves when I walked in the room, but one was a little warmer than the rest. She was tall and thin with dark brown hair. Her eyes seemed to disappear when she smiled, which was often—but mine did too, so I didn't mind. I liked that she had the guts to talk to me when most of her friends treated me like a leper. Eventually, I asked her to hang out with me at a park near our apartment. It was cold out, but I barely noticed because of how present and inviting she was. She listened to what I was feeling at the time—the isolation from my peers and the anxiety of trying to figure out how to eventually support myself—and told me the same from her side. While we were there, I drew a portrait of her. I sent it to her later.

She invited me to meet her close friends.

I realized she may have been interested in me, and I didn't know how to handle it. Sure, I'd had casual "relationships" with people who didn't look like me. And sure, I'd met women from other ethnic groups and wanted to bring them home to my parents but couldn't. But this was the first time someone I took seriously was returning the favor. Something about that—sitting at that diner in Brooklyn with her childhood friends, a half step away from a train ride to her White household—scared me. I was cold to her that night. When she tried to touch my hand under the table, I drew it back into my coat pocket. And when she asked me questions about my family or my childhood in order to clue her friends in, I gave short answers and looked at the door rather than at her. Her friends could tell that something was off and offered to walk her home. I went with them, and one of them gave me the evil eye the whole time. I must have seemed dangerous.

Soon after that, we had one of our loft parties. I invited the girl I'd drawn. We hadn't communicated much after that night with her friends, but I wanted a second chance. I started drinking before the sun went down. People showed up. I looked for the girl. She didn't show, so I drank. My model roommate brought hundreds of gold chocolate coins from the Alexander Wang after-party and scattered them across the floor. His girlfriend had a Polaroid OneStep and took individual portraits of each one of our mutual friends except for me.

More people showed up. I looked for the girl. She still didn't show, so I drank more. A local musician who was friends with the French girl played a set amid twinkling Christmas lights and a crowd that was surging by the minute. I danced on top of the wooden coffee table I'd purchased at IKEA until it fell in on itself and cut me.

More people showed up. I tried to forget about the girl but couldn't. I drank more. There were plenty of young women there— cute ones too, in miniskirts and halter tops—but I was waiting for the one I'd invited. It became apparent that she wasn't going to show up at all. I started breaking bottles against the kitchen floor like the overgrown child I was. A few friends joined in. My roommate made us stop. His face went red as the people who were friends with him but whispered about "that black kid from North Carolina" in the hallways of our school looked on.

People started to leave. I would've drunk more if I weren't busy being drunk. Part of the party and I spilled out into the hallway, where we mixed and mingled with another party that was going on next door. We'd switched to punk music. The guitar was driving at points and frenetic at others. The lyrics were undecipherable. I was on my way back in when somebody pushed me. I hit him. Then I felt a wave of hands grip me and shove me out of my apartment. The door slammed in my face. I went downstairs to a friend's apartment. I was furious, but he calmed me down and told me that from the sound of the footsteps coming through his ceiling, I'd walked into the middle of an impromptu mosh pit and it was all just a misunderstanding. Then I went back upstairs and knocked on the door. I could hear that the party had ended, and I just wanted to go to sleep.

"Go away!" I heard from one of my roommates.

"Dude, let me in!"

"You fucking embarrassed all of us tonight. I don't want to live with you!"

"That's fine, but my name is on the lease—let me in!"

"The cops came because of you!"

"They've been here all night—there were four parties going on! Let me in!"

I kicked the door. The hinges buckled. I kicked it again, then I heard it unlock. It opened. I stepped through and then felt the blunt force of a closed fist against my left eye. I flew backward against the white wall opposite our apartment.

"Nigger," I heard as I tried to keep upright. The word meant there was no going back. The door slammed and locked again as my face began to swell. I went downstairs to see if my superintendent had an ice pack or a key or both.

I STOPPED REMEMBERING and began to look around. The recollection had only taken a few moments. All I really heard in my head was the way the word had rolled off of each speaker's tongue. I started to see the scene before me as it unfolded itself. I was out there on that hot summer day in New York, standing in the middle of Tompkins Square Park in my Curry 1s with my pizza in the trash can and something nasty on the tip of my tongue.

Maybe I wouldn't have said it if I hadn't been so dejected. But the memories of pain and rejection hung over me like a spirit that never received proper burial rites. I'd gotten too many interviews over the phone that led to shocked looks in person, loose handshakes, and *we'll call you*s. Too many people slid over when I sat next to them on crowded subway trains. I'd heard too many headlines about Black boys and men being gunned down in the streets that didn't directly pertain to me but somehow felt as if they could have included my name in place of the victim of the day's.

I'd been reduced to a stereotype—someone who woke up without an alarm clock, hung out by the basketball court, drank to forget, and did it all again without thinking twice about why or how or for how long that could last. I'd been reduced to that word they called me—the one I heard on my first day at my first job, the one the kid called me at summer camp, the one my play uncles used in jest, the one that was a threat of violence but never ceased to be violent in and of itself, the one I bled to that night in Brooklyn, the one I'd never said before.

I looked over at Bo Jackson Jr. with the basketball in his hand.

I opened my mouth.

I squared my shoulders.

And I let it fly.

"*Nigga*, if you don't give me that damn ball!"

He looked at me, wide-eyed.

All of the lost love and shared hopelessness and dismal kinship was sent out into the hot summer air. It bounced off of the ozone until it pressed back down on everyone within earshot with enough force and power to melt a press or make the air in front of you ripple like a puddle in a rainstorm. I stood and sounded like a man, and yet I felt a piece of my humanity leaving my body. I saw the yoke that my ancestors once wore, how it connected them by the neck and shoulders. I saw the chains that bound them at the ankles in steerage. I formed my own wireless connection, volatile, with sparks like a Tesla coil. And it threatened my vitality but made me feel free.

"My bad," he said. "You got next with ol' boy over there."

Isaac Hughes Green attended the North Carolina State University MFA program and NYU Tisch, has been published in *The Georgia Review*, and won the 2021 Jacobs/Jones African-American Literary Prize, in addition to being longlisted for *The Masters Review*'s 2019 Fall Fiction contest and receiving honorable mention for the 2019 James Hurst Prize for Fiction. Green screened a film in the Cannes Short Film Corner and has won screenwriting and cinematography awards. He centers diversity in his writing.

ABOUT THE JUDGES

NANA KWAME ADJEI-BRENYAH is the *New York Times* bestselling author of *Friday Black*. Originally from Spring Valley, New York, he graduated from SUNY Albany and went on to receive his MFA from Syracuse University. His work has appeared in numerous publications, including *Esquire, Literary Hub, The Paris Review, Guernica,* and *Longreads*. He was selected by Colson Whitehead as one of the National Book Foundation's "5 Under 35" honorees.

KALI FAJARDO-ANSTINE is the author of *Sabrina & Corina*, a finalist for the National Book Award, the PEN/Bingham Prize, The Story Prize, and winner of a 2020 American Book Award. She is the 2021 recipient of the Addison M. Metcalf Award from the American Academy of Arts and Letters. Her writing has appeared in numerous publications, such as *The New York Times, Harper's Bazaar, Elle, O, The Oprah Magazine,* and *The American Scholar*. Her stories have been translated into numerous languages.

BETH PIATOTE is the author of the mixed-genre collection *The Beadworkers: Stories*, which was long listed for the PEN/Robert W. Bingham Prize for Debut Short Story Collection and the Aspen Words Literary Prize, and short-listed for the California Independent Bookselller Alliance "Golden Poppy" Award in Fiction. Her short stories, poems, and essays have appeared in *Kenyon Review, Catapult, Moss,* and numerous journals and anthologies. She is Nez Perce enrolled with the Confederated Tribes of the Colville Reservation.

ABOUT THE PEN/ROBERT J. DAU SHORT STORY PRIZE FOR EMERGING WRITERS

THE PEN/ROBERT J. Dau Short Story Prize for Emerging Writers recognizes twelve fiction writers for a debut short story published in a print or online literary magazine. The annual award was offered for the first time during PEN America's 2017 literary awards cycle.

The twelve winning stories are selected by a committee of three judges. The writers of the stories each receive a $2,000 cash prize and are honored at the annual PEN America Literary Awards Ceremony in New York City. Every year, Catapult publishes the winning stories in *Best Debut Short Stories: The PEN America Dau Prize*.

This award is generously supported by the family of the late Robert J. Dau, whose commitment to the literary arts has made him a fitting namesake for this career-launching prize. Mr. Dau was born and raised in Petoskey, a city in Northern Michigan in close proximity to Walloon Lake, where Ernest Hemingway had spent his summers as a young boy and which serves as the backdrop for Hemingway's *The Torrents of Spring*. Petoskey is also known for being where Hemingway determined that he would commit to becoming a writer. This proximity to literary history ignited the Dau family's interest in promoting emerging voices in fiction and spotlighting the next great fiction writers.

LIST OF PARTICIPATING PUBLICATIONS

PEN America and Catapult gratefully acknowledge the following publications, which published debut fiction in 2020 and submitted work for consideration to the PEN/Robert J. Dau Short Story Prize.

3Elements Literary Review
805 Lit + Art
adda
AGNI
American Short Fiction
Barrelhouse
Berkeley Fiction Review
Black Warrior Review
Boston Review
Brio Literary Journal
Carve Magazine
Change Seven
Columbia Journal
The Common
The Conium Review
The Courtship of Winds
Defunkt Magazine
Dispatches
Down River Road

Driftwood Press

Dristikon

Electric Literature's Recommended Reading

Electric Literature's The Commuter

English Bay Review

Epiphany Magazine

Evergreen Review

Exposition Review

Fairy Tale Review

Five Points

Foglifter

Forever Endeavour Magazine

The Forge Literary Magazine

Four Way Review

GASHER Journal

The Georgia Review

The Gettysburg Review

Granta

The Gravity of the Thing

Gulf Coast: A Journal of Literature and Fine Arts

Hypertext Review

The Ilanot Review

International Human Rights Art Festival

Kestrel: A Journal of Literature and Art

Lightspeed Magazine

The Literary Review

The Lit Quarterly

Lit Star Review

The Los Angeles Review

McSweeney's

Memorious

Mensa Bulletin

Michigan Quarterly Review

midnight & indigo

Midwest Review

Muumuu House

New England Review

Newfound

The New Yorker

New York Tyrant Magazine

Nimrod International Journal

NOON

Nowhere Magazine

October Hill Magazine

Okay Donkey Magazine

Orca

Oxford American

Oyez Review

Oyster River Pages

PANK

Pigeon Pages

Ploughshares

Porter House Review

Prospectus: A Literary Offering

Puerto del Sol

Roars & Whispers

The Rumpus

The Rupture

Salamander

sinθ magazine
So to Speak
The Southern Review
Southwest Review
The Summerset Review
SUNU: Journal of African Affairs, Critical Thought + Aesthetics
The Threepenny Review
Timeworn Literary Journal
Virginia Quarterly Review
Washington Square Review
Waxwing Magazine
West Branch
Westerly Magazine
Wild Roof Journal
Wordrunner eChapbooks

PERMISSIONS

PEN America stands at the intersection of literature and human rights to protect open expression in the United States and worldwide. The organization champions the freedom to write, recognizing the power of the word to transform the world. Its mission is to unite writers and their allies to celebrate creative expression and defend the liberties that make it possible. Learn more at pen.org.